This dark climb lacked the assistance of fabricated hand-holds and a belay rope. Finding firm holds on the rough dirt wall wasn't easy. But I couldn't give up.

My arms stretched high and I fumbled around for something solid to grab. Dirt crumbled. My fingers slipped. I tried again, grasping a jutting rock, using my strength to pull myself high, gripping a dangling root next, then another rock, until my head bumped something solid.

I'd reached the top!

But a heavy obstruction blocked the opening. Feeling the rough, hard object, I realized it was a concrete slab, like a cork bottling me alive inside the dirt hole. How had the concrete gotten there? Heavy slabs didn't just appear.

Someone had covered the hole.

Trapping me inside.

On purpose.

Don't miss the other books in the series!

ReGeneration

THE SEARCH

ReGeneration

The Truth

L. J. Singleton

BERKLEY JAM BOOKS, NEW YORK

REGENERATION: THE TRUTH

A Berkley Jam Book / published by arrangement with
the author

PRINTING HISTORY
Berkley Jam edition / May 2000

The Penguin Putnam Inc. World Wide Web site address is
http://www.penguinputnam.com

ISBN: 0-425-17415-8

BERKLEY JAM BOOKS®
Berkley Jam Books are published by The Berkley Publishing Group,
a division of Penguin Putnam Inc.,
375 Hudson Street, New York, New York 10014.
BERKLEY JAM and its logo are trademarks
belonging to Penguin Putnam Inc.

PRINTED IN THE UNITED STATES OF AMERICA

10 9 8 7 6 5 4 3 2

Thanks to the fun and helpful members of my on-line critique group, Dreamers.

Melody DeLeons
Gail Martini-Peterson
Miriam Hees
Jan LaBrenz
Kathy Rappaho
Robin Clifton
Jennifer Reed
Dona Vaughn
Shirley Harazin
Judy Gregerson

Dear DNA Donor
To My Genetic Parent
Hey, Bio-Mom!
Dear Ms. Cressida Ray, International Model
Ms. Ray

Dear Cressida,

You don't know me, but I know about you. I am your clone.
Does that make me your daughter, sister, twin, or YOU?

You don't know me, but I recently learned about you.

I can't believe you're a model, because we share the same
genes and yet I HATE modeling. Not that it's a bad job,
just bor-ring. Sitting still for hours must be very hard. Still,
it's SO neat you're famous and successful. And I'd really love
to meet you.

I would love to meet you.

There are SO many questions I'm dying to ask you! Like,
do you enjoy peanut butter and pickle sandwiches? Do roman-
tic movies make you cry? Do you wish your straight hair was
naturally curly? And is the little toe on your right foot
crooked like mine? I bet we have A LOT in common.

I bet we have a lot in common.

I saw your picture in an old magazine, not that I'm saying you're old. Although you have to be at least forty, right?
Anyway, when I saw your picture I knew you were THE ONE.
My clone. See, I was born in a weird experiment over fifteen
years ago, but I only found out last fall. And when I saw
you on that magazine, and realized we were total duplicates,
I knew my DNA came from you.

My picture is enclosed.

sincerely,

Allison Lynn Beaumont

ONE

"More nails, please!" I shouted, after searching my overalls pockets and finding only a few screws, a wad of chewed gum, and some sunflower seeds.

Around me, the construction site clamored with volunteers and professionals working together. Hammers pounded, shovels clanged, and machinery rumbled the contented purr of heavy equipment. It was Saturday, a day most people relaxed or enjoyed a movie, but not our group. We were building a home for a needy family.

"SOS over here!" I stood awkwardly, with one hand raised high to hold a 4×8 header over a doorway and the other hand searching for a nail. I looked around, blinking into the bright March sunshine. "Hey, anyone! I need a nail!"

Just my luck, "anyone" turned out to be Dustin Stratton-Butterfield, or as I'd nicknamed him: Dusty Stiff-Bottom. Some girls at school oohed and aahed and called him a hunk, but I wasn't fooled by his pretty face. He was a major pain in the rear. And lately he'd been hanging around *me*.

"Allison, did you say you needed a *male*?" Dustin flashed a pearly-white smile and gave an exaggerated bow. "Here I am."

"Not a *male*. A *nail*." I gnashed my teeth, fighting to keep my cool. I'd met plenty of arrogant guys like Dustin. Growing up around a wealthy, political crowd, I'd had a childhood filled with pompous, social-climbing creeps. And unfortunately, like a dog attracted fleas, I attracts flea-brains like Dustin.

"Oh, a *nail*!" He chuckled, digging into his leather work belt and handing me a nail. "Why didn't you say something? Here."

Glaring, I snatched the nail and then withdrew my hammer from my belt loop and smacked the nail in. I imagined Dustin's face on the nail and pounded so hard the 4×8 cracked and then split in two. Oops! I'd forgotten my own strength.

"How'd you do that?" Dustin's jaw sagged open. "That's incredible!"

"The board must have had a flaw," I said evasively. Dustin was the last person I wanted to let in on my secret.

"That must have been *some* flaw. It snapped like a twig."

"Just a freak accident." I glanced over to where a group of volunteers were shoveling dirt into a wheelbarrow. "Uh, you'd better go back to wheelbarrow duty. I'll get another board."

"Uh . . ." He pushed his longish, dark brown hair away from his blue eyes. "Yeah, I guess I better get back . . . but I still can't believe . . ." His words trailed off as he shook his head. He gave me one last suspicious look, then left to join the wheelbarrow crew.

"That was close," I murmured, letting out a sigh. Then I surveyed the damaged board and felt ashamed of myself. I'd almost blown it big-time. My friends Varina and Eric had warned me to hide my unusual strength. But sometimes that was so hard.

I'd always been the kind of person who said what was on my mind and did whatever popped into my head. Keeping secrets was not in my DNA. But then my DNA was the whole reason for secrecy.

I mean, how many fifteen-year-old girls were CLONES?

It wasn't the kind of news you could just shout out to the world. How would anyone react to "Hey, guess what! "I don't have two parents and I wasn't born in a hospital. I was mixed in a tube in a secret experiment on a yacht. And since turning thirteen, I've developed amazing strength. I could lift up this whole building if I wanted."

Imagining how this announcement would shock everyone, including my parents, I smiled to myself. Then I replaced the broken board, found a box of nails, and resumed hammering.

I marveled how much my life had changed since I'd learned I was a clone. I no longer lived at the Pacific Palace for Young Ladies, which I'd nicknamed "Prissy Prison." I'd been thrilled to move in with my new "clone family": Varina Fergus, her uncle Professor Jim Fergus, and Eric Prince. Varina and Eric had been cloned in secret like me, and Professor Fergus was one of the doctors who'd created us.

To avoid questions, Professor Fergus had officially opened a "Tutorial School for Gifted Students." It was a school in name only; a means to live together without awkward questions. Varina, Eric, and I were the only students, but I hoped the two remaining clones, Chase and Sandee, would join soon.

Moving in with the Ferguses hadn't been easy. At first my parents hated the idea. But they gave in after I threatened to tell the media that Congressman Beaumont had illegally adopted his daughter. They didn't know about my genetic past, but they did know a rebellious daughter was poison for a political career.

Of course, I wouldn't really have blabbed to the press. And instead of feeling triumphant, I felt let down. Father seemed relieved to let me go, and Mother was always involved with her charity events, so I was only an afterthought to her anyway. She'd once told a friend she loved me "more than life itself," but the truth was she didn't even *like* me.

Sometimes this hurt, like when Mother boasted in an interview that I was a straight-A student who enjoyed campaigning for my father and aspired to follow in his political footsteps. *Lies.* I barely kept a B average and I resented politics. But I'd never measured up to my parents' expectations. So years ago, I'd stopped trying.

Not that I felt sorry for myself. No way! If I couldn't find a family at home, then I'd find one with friends like Varina and Eric. And when I graduated from high school, I would pursue my dream to enter a construction apprentice program.

I held the new 4×8 high and smacked the last nail firmly into the wood. All done! Now what would I work on?

Hearing a metallic clink, I turned to glance at a slender, cocoa-skinned girl with wild beads in her black braids.

Starr Montgomery wiped grime from her cheek as she shoveled dirt into a wheelbarrow. Starr was Varina's best friend, so I'd met her on my first day at Seymore High. It had been a surprise to see way-cool, ultra-popular Starr dirtying herself on a construction site. A *nice* surprise.

Starr looked up and waved at me. "Hey, Allison!"

"How's it going?" I asked as I walked toward her.

"Not bad. But I need a break." She smoothed back her braids. "Want to take over for me?"

"Sure. I finished my job."

"Great. Here!" Starr grabbed her shovel and suddenly threw it to me. "Catch!"

I raised my arms and reached for the shovel, but as I turned, the sun flashed on my face and instinctively I closed my eyes. Crash! The shovel slipped through my hands and banged my foot.

"Ouch!" I cried, hopping on one foot.

"Hey, I'm really sorry." Starr bent down to pick up the shovel with an apologetic half-smile. "You're usually so athletic. I thought you'd catch it."

I lifted my hand to shade my eyes from the sun's glare. "I thought I'd catch it, too."

"Your foot okay?"

"I think so." I put my weight on it, then winced at the sudden pain. Those cloned genes that gave me super strength didn't prevent me from having cuts and bruises.

"Hey, girlfriend, no need to hop around. Listen to Mother Starr now, and take a break. Better take off your shoe to make sure you aren't bleeding. Go sit on that bench over there." She pointed to a far corner of the half-finished garage. Boxes of nails and roofing material were stacked against a garage wall, as well as scattered across the rooftop.

"Maybe I will." I limped after her. "But just for a few minutes. I don't want anyone calling me a slacker."

"Not a chance. No one works as hard as you. And you never seem to get tired."

"I guess I have good genes," I said with a secret smile.

"Think I'll take a break, too." Starr grinned. "If that pesky Dustin tries to boss me around some more, I might forget I'm a lady and smash a shovel on his head."

"Only a shovel?" I teased.

"Too small? How about a bulldozer?"

"Better. But Dustin's skull is so thick, he probably wouldn't notice."

"Darned straight!" Starr laughed. "That jerk acts like

he's in charge. If he tells me to work faster one more time, I'm going to find a bulldozer."

"He's too pushy."

"Like Hitler with dimples." Sitting down on the rough wooden bench, Starr gave a long sigh. "He's really fine-looking, too. If only he wasn't such a . . ." She bent forward and then whispered the *perfect* word to describe Dusty Stiff-Bottom—not a word I could repeat, either.

When we stopped laughing, Starr leaned forward with a conspiratorial grin. "Guess who I'm gonna ask to the Sadie Hawkins Dance?"

"Alonzo?"

"Nope. He's yesterday. Got too possessive and pulled some macho attitudes. So I'm looking for a different kind of guy." Her black eyes sparkled as she lowered her voice in a gossipy whisper. "And I think I've found him."

"That's great!" I untied my shoe and rolled down my sock to check my foot. No blood, just the beginning of a dark bruise. "Anyone I know?"

She nodded.

"What grade's he in?"

"Ninth."

"A freshman!" I nearly fell off the bench, shocked that sophomore vice president Starr would go for a lowly freshman. "But he's younger than you. My age!"

"Age isn't everything. He's so mature, and real polite, too." Her face lit up like sunshine. "He's the classy type who'll bring flowers, rent a tux, and escort me to the dance in a limo like that shiny one I saw earlier. And he's cute, too. I love the way he stretches out his words in that cute accent—"

"Accent?"

"Yup." Starr smiled proudly. "Texas guys sound so sexy."

"Texas! Geez!" I exclaimed. "You don't mean—"

Before I could finish my sentence, there was a loud

sound from the garage roof. I glanced up to see a flash of orange and a dark shape. Then a heavy bundle of roof shakes was falling—plunging directly toward ME!

It seemed to happen in slow motion, and there was barely time to move out of the way. I dodged sideways and reached up with both hands, but I wasn't quick enough.

The shakes crashed.

I screamed, and felt pain.

Dirt and dust exploded as I fell to the ground.

TWO

I blinked at Starr's concerned face hovering over me. My palms stung and my heart pounded. The roofing bundle had missed my head but had crashed against my hands.

"Can you move?" Starr was asking, her beaded braids rattling over my face.

"Yeah." I looked down at my scraped, red palms. "But my hands hurt."

"Of course they do. That bundle was heavy." Starr carefully eased me upright on the bench. "It would have clobbered you on the head if you hadn't moved just in time."

Dustin came rushing over. "I saw what happened!" he exclaimed. "Allison, are you okay?"

"Uh huh." I nodded as my nose tickled and I sneezed.

"You don't look good. I'd better call 911. Or better yet, Starr can use my cell phone to make the call."

"Me?" Starr frowned. "But she's not bleeding or anything."

"She might have internal injuries. That bundle

weighed at least eighty pounds! Allison could have been killed!"

"But I'm okay. I definitely don't need an ambulance," I protested. My hands ached, but the pain had lessened to a dull throb. I saw a few other members of the construction crew heading my way, so I stood up and wiped the dirt from my face.

"What happened here?" a short guy named Arnold Sayid asked. He was the site foreman, although Starr once joked he looked more like an accountant than a construction worker.

"I saw it all," Dustin spoke up. "That clumsy jerk on the roof knocked down a bundle of shakes."

"Yeah." I remembered the flash of orange I'd seen. "There was someone on the roof."

"Some guy in an orange cap and black coat," Dustin added.

"Who?" Arnold rubbed his stubby beard and peered up at the empty garage roof. "No one's working there today."

"Well, someone was there." Dustin scowled. "I want him kicked off this site. He's a total menace."

"Orange cap and black coat?" Arnold looked around at the small crowd who'd gathered. "You must be mistaken. No one here fits that description."

"But I saw him. He was up there." Dustin pointed toward the roof. "He must have run off after he almost killed Allison. You know, Allison's father is an important congressman. . . ."

Dustin's words were ignored as Arnold turned to question me. But I couldn't tell him much. It had happened so fast, my brain hadn't caught up with my memory yet. Although . . . I felt an odd nagging sensation, like I'd seen something else . . . something strange . . . but I had no idea what.

Thinking about those plummeting shakes made my legs rubbery, and my heart pounded anxiously. I gritted my teeth and assured myself that it had been an accident and there was no reason to be afraid. Maybe I looked fragile with my blond hair and pale skin, but I was made of tougher stuff. And I refused to be treated like a child.

"I'm fine," I stated with a determined lift of my chin. "I'll go home and get some rest. Don't worry about me."

The foreman argued that I should go to the hospital, but I refused. Sure I was sore and bruised, but otherwise I felt okay. It had been a freak accident and I just wanted to forget it.

Starr was going to call her mother to pick us both up, but when Dustin said he would drive us, it was an offer too convenient to refuse.

Starr and I left in Dustin's sporty red Mustang. Dustin told Starr to sit in the back, and then invited me to sit up front. As he helped me inside, his hand lingered on mine far too long. Yuck! Did he actually think I liked him that way? *Not even!*

The short drive seemed long with Dustin spouting off about his high grade-point average and all the college invitation letters he had received in the mail. Of course, he'd thrown away the letters from small, unimportant colleges. His collegiate goals were targeted on only the most prestigious colleges. Anything less than Harvard or Yale was an insult to his accomplishments.

Listening to Dustin rattle on was an insult to *my sensibilities.* I leaned back against the seat and closed my eyes, but Dustin didn't get the hint. By the time we reached my new home, I was ready to throw a bundle of shakes on *his* head. Anything to shut him up.

"Thanks for the ride," Starr said, rolling her eyes. "Go on back. I'll make sure Allison's okay."

She stepped out of the car, then reached over to give me a hand. As I stepped forward, pain flared from my foot, causing me to double in pain.

Immediately, Dustin was by my side, trying way too hard to be a gentleman, helping me into the house.

"Lean against me, Allison," Dustin said, holding my arm as we stepped into the tiled foyer. He glanced toward the living room and added, "Nice place, but it could use more furniture."

"They just moved here," Starr told him sarcastically. "Any moron could figure that out from the unpacked boxes and empty walls. Besides, it's not Allison's house anyway."

"So whose house is it?"

"Varina Fergus and her uncle own it. Allison boards with Professor Fergus for private tutoring. Not that it's any of your business."

"Professor James Fergus?" Dustin's expression sharpened with interest. "I used one of his scientific articles for an honors biology report. And Varina is his niece? Cool! Maybe I'll sign up for some tutoring."

"Don't waste your time," Starr snapped. "He only takes on special students."

"Special in what way?"

"Uh, you better leave," I interrupted quickly.

"Yeah. But I want to hear more about your tutoring. What's the deal?" Dustin asked suspiciously.

"Nothing. I'm really tired and I'm going to lie down. Thanks for taking me home."

"I get the hint. I'll leave, but we'll talk about this later." He narrowed his gaze at me, then whirled around and strode out of the house.

Starr looked at me and shook her head. "You're whiter than chalk. Maybe you *should* go to the hospital."

"No way. I'll be okay."

"But just to be safe, Varina's uncle should check you out. He's a doctor, isn't he?"

"Not *that* kind of doctor. A professor of science. And he's probably busy in his office, so I don't want to bother him. I just need to sit down."

Starr followed me into the living room and eased me into a cushioned chair. "Are you feeling better?"

I nodded, but it was only a half-truth. Physically I *was* better. The pain in my hands had dulled, but a sudden memory shook me.

Leaning against the soft cushion, I closed my eyes and relived the accident: chatting on the bench with Starr, hearing a sudden sound, glancing up and seeing the flash of orange and then a dark shape. Only now I clearly remembered that the dark shape was a person; a person with pale hands that reached for the bundle of shakes.

I was sure now that my accident hadn't been an accident at all.

THREE

I fought down panic.

Who had tried to kill me? And why?

Did it have anything to do with my being a clone?

I must have been zoning, because when I glanced up, Starr was staring at me. Her hands were planted on her hips and she pursed her full, mauve-painted lips curiously. "What's wrong?"

"Nothing." I glanced away, afraid she might guess I was lying. "My hands and feet are just aching."

"You *are* in pain. Why didn't you just say so?" Instantly, Starr was by my side, all sympathetic. "Oh, you poor thing."

"Who's a poor thing?" a boyish voice with a soft Texas drawl asked, coming from the hallway. Dark-skinned, ebony-eyed Eric breezed into the room. He joked, "No way are *you* poor, Allison. You're the richest girl I know."

"Not bank-account poor." Starr's words held more syrup than sting. Her gaze settled on Eric, and she smiled warmly. "I'm glad you're here. Allison needs good friends like us right now."

"Why?" Eric pushed his glasses up on his nose and gave me a startled look. "What happened?"

"Nothing really," I began to say. But Starr was already launching into an overly dramatic version of the accident. And somehow *she* was the heroine of the story while I was merely a walk-on character. I couldn't help but grin. Starr was so obvious, and yet Eric didn't seem to have a clue.

"Starr, you were great to help Allison." Eric stared into Starr's eyes, his tone polite and respectful. Being raised in a large Texan family had given him wonderful manners. No wonder Starr wanted to go out with him.

"I'm always there for my friends." The way Starr said "friends" was full of deep meaning. I knew it wouldn't take long for her to reel Eric in, hook, line, and Sadie Hawkins Dance.

They continued to gaze at each other, until Starr happened to glance at her watch. "Shoot! I didn't realize it was so late."

"You have to go?" Eric asked, disappointed.

"Yeah. See, Grandma has this big date tonight with a younger man—he's only eighty-six—and I promised to dye her hair. I'm thinking pink or green. But knowing Grandma, she may want peach again. The color really brings out the tiger tattoo on her shoulder." Starr gave a sparkling laugh and then smiled seductively at Eric. "We'll talk later. You have my number?"

"Not yet." Eric returned the smile. "But I know where to get it. Would you like me to walk you home?"

"Oh, I'd like. But I only live a few blocks away, not very far, and you should stay with Allison." Then she waved and left.

Once the door closed behind Starr, Eric stared for a moment with a goofy smile on his face. Then he turned to me, his expression growing serious. "Okay, Allison. Out with it."

"Out with what?"

"What really happened?"

I hesitated, knowing I couldn't fool Eric. We'd been through a lot together: learning about our unusual powers, rescuing his sister, and becoming close friends. "It's not that big of a deal. Just a freak accident. A bundle of roof shakes fell toward me and scraped my hands."

He leaned over to look at my hands and frowned. "With your strength you could have swatted those shakes away like flies. Why didn't you?"

"It happened so quick. And I was startled by something I saw." I sunk deeper into the cushioned chair as I stared at my bruised hands. "There was someone on the roof with pale hands. I—I think he tried to kill me."

"Geez, that's horrible. But don't worry, we'll figure out what's going on." Eric pulled over one of the large unpacked moving boxes and sat on the edge of it, so we were face-to-face. "Remember your nickname for us clones?"

"C.C.'s."

"Yeah. And that's what we are. Clone cousins who stick together." Eric reached out to playfully tug my long braid. "We'll find that creep who tried to hurt you."

"I hope so."

"Have you told Uncle Jim?"

"Nope. I only just got home. I haven't seen Professor Fergus yet." It might have been easy for Eric to call Professor Fergus "Uncle Jim," but not me. I hadn't even been allowed to call my own mother "Mom." That word was too childish, in her opinion.

"Uncle Jim is in his office," Eric said. "We better tell him."

"But if he gets upset, it might cause another migraine. His health still isn't good, and I don't want to add any stress."

Last fall, Professor Fergus had lapsed into a coma after being attacked during a break-in. Although it had never been proven, we knew his former associate Dr. Victor was behind it all. Dr. Victor had been involved in the secret cloning experiment, but now he wanted all of us clones dead.

I wondered if Dr. Victor was responsible for my accident. But that didn't seem likely. The last time he'd threatened us, he'd been shot in the foot and arrested. Since getting out of jail, he'd kept a low profile. Instead it was his wife, Geneva, who targeted us. She was a greedy witch with dollar signs for a heart, and I still had nightmares from our last encounter.

But would either of the Victors risk climbing onto a roof in public to drop a heavy bundle on me? I doubted it. Besides, my assailant had pale hands, not dark skin like Dr. Victor. And Geneva was petite, so that eliminated her as a suspect, too.

"Allison, you have to talk to Uncle Jim," Eric was saying.

"Yeah, I know I should. I will later."

"Don't put it off. Someone has to make you take care of yourself. Come on, let's go tell him now." Eric stood up and reached for my hand, but I just sat there with my arms pressed against the chair.

"Stop being stubborn. Remember what Uncle Jim said when he invited us to move here?"

I pursed my lips unresponsively, but I remembered all too well. Professor Fergus had looked so frail, leaning on his cane, his jagged scar a white streak over his right eyebrow. He started off by admitting he couldn't tell us much about our pasts. "The less you know, the safer you are," he'd warned. Even though we'd asked a zillion questions about our DNA donors and the clone experiment, he wouldn't answer. Instead, he offered to help us understand our powers.

But there were two conditions for living here.

#1: We keep the fact that we were clones a secret.

#2: We tell Professor Fergus if anything unusual happens.

Like nearly getting bashed on the head, I realized with a stab of guilt.

"You win, Eric." I sighed. "Let's go find him."

We walked down the hall, pausing by the arched opening of the kitchen. I noticed the stack of mail on a counter. "Wait a sec, Eric. I've got to check on something."

"What? Oh, the mail." His dark brows arched knowingly. "I already checked it today. No letters for me from Texas or for you from—"

"Shssh!" I cautioned, my finger to my lips. "Don't say her name. You promised to keep my letter a secret."

"No one can hear us."

"It doesn't hurt to be careful." I went over to the counter and flipped through the bills, letters, and sales ads, but found nothing addressed to me. Darn.

"I told you there wasn't anything."

"Yeah. Still . . ." I paused, wishing there were an easy way to put my hopes into words. With busy parents like mine, I could sure use someone who understood me. And who better than my own clone, Cressida Ray? She was me. Or maybe I was her. The whole concept of cloning was *so* confusing.

"Eric, I've been wondering . . ." I hesitated, biting my lip as I met his sincere, dark-eyed gaze.

"What?" He grabbed a can of cherry soda from the fridge, then turned to face me.

"It's been a month since I sent the letter, and I keep thinking." I blew out a deep breath of air. "Was it a mistake to write to her?"

"I don't know." He popped open the soda and shrugged. "I couldn't care less about my genetic donor. Somewhere there's a grown-up Eric who shares my DNA, but our birth was a big secret so he probably doesn't even know I exist."

"Maybe I shouldn't have written the letter. She probably took one look at my letter, then tossed it out with the junk mail."

"No." Eric shook his head. "She wouldn't do that."

"How can you know?"

"Because she's like you. Maybe she's impulsive and hotheaded, but she wouldn't be cruel. Never." Eric reached out to squeeze my hand. I winced.

"Sorry. I didn't mean to hurt you."

"It's okay. It didn't hurt."

"Can't you just admit you're in pain?" He shook his head with a rueful smile. "You're impossible sometimes."

"Only sometimes?" I teased. "I'll have to work harder."

"Quit stalling. Let's talk to Uncle Jim."

"Okay. And Eric," I added softly. "Thanks."

We headed down the hall to the large room that Professor Fergus used as a combination office/lab. Varina was the only one allowed in on a regular basis, since she helped with filing and light paperwork. She was really into science and enjoyed biological articles and experiments—stuff that seemed pretty dull to me.

After tapping on the door and hearing a gruff "Come in," I wasn't surprised to see Varina sitting cross-legged on the floor in the center of scattered stacks of files and papers.

"I can't find the maize reproduction article," Varina told her uncle, pushing back her wavy auburn hair. "It's not here."

"It has to be." Her uncle reached for his cane and then shakily stood up from his desk. He leaned against the cane, pausing to catch his breath, and I felt a stab of worry about his health.

"Good afternoon, Eric and Allison." Professor Fergus rubbed his graying beard and smiled. "Why don't you two give Varina a hand. It's imperative I find that research paper."

Eric cleared his throat. "Can't we talk first?"

Varina stopped sorting papers and glanced up. "Is something wrong?"

"Not exactly . . ." I hid my bruised hands behind my back.

"Then it can wait a minute," Professor Fergus said, still searching his desk. "As soon as I find that paper—" As he said the word "paper," the phone rang.

"But Uncle Jim—," Eric started to say, only Professor Fergus was already reaching for the phone.

"Good afternoon. Fergus here." He paused to listen, then gave a harsh gasp. His hands shook. And the pen he'd been holding dropped to the desk with a sharp *ping*.

"YOU!" he choked out. "Why the hell are you calling here?"

FOUR

Varina, Eric, and I stared in astonishment at Professor Fergus. His knuckles on the receiver were bone-white and his face was mottled red with fury. I'd never seen him so enraged.

"NO!" Professor Fergus spat out. "I will not listen to any offer from you!"

Varina crossed the room and gently touched her uncle's arm. "What's wrong? Who is it?"

He ignored his niece and unleashed a storm of angry words into the phone. "I can't believe you have the gall to call here. You're a double-crosser and a murderer. Don't deny it. I'm sure you caused the death of Chase's parents!"

I shared stunned glances with Varina and Eric. The caller *had* to be Dr. Victor or his wife, Geneva. Separately they were dangerous, together they were deadly.

"What?" Professor Fergus cried as if he'd been struck. "I don't care how much you're willing to pay for it, I'm not interested. . . . NO!"

Professor Fergus gave a strangled gasp, then collapsed

into his chair, clutching the phone. He seemed to be listening, but said nothing. His silence was even more frightening than his anger. When he finally spoke again, his voice was an anguished whisper. "I don't believe it. *Not her.* You can't possibly know after all these years. . . . Just leave her alone!"

Then he slammed down the phone, shaking his head and murmuring one word: Jessica.

"So who's Jessica?" I asked Varina a short time later.

Eric, Varina, and I were sitting around TV trays with frozen pizzas in the living room. Professor Fergus had been so upset, he'd ordered us out of his office and locked the door.

Varina didn't answer right away, but I could tell from her tight lips and the tense set of her shoulders that she recognized the name. And it was obviously someone who meant a lot to her.

"Was Jessica the name of Uncle Jim's sister?" Eric asked, wiping mozzarella cheese from his chin with a napkin.

"No." Varina's green eyes grew moist. "Uncle Jim's sister and her husband died in a train wreck when I was little. I used to think they were my real parents until I found out about the cloning. Dr. Jessica Hart was involved in that experiment."

"Dr. Hart?" I recognized that name. She was one of the doctors on the yacht who'd created clones. I'd only been a baby and didn't remember her at all, but Professor Fergus had described the fateful night when he and Dr. Hart had rescued us. While Dr. Hart was getting into the escape boat, Dr. Victor shot her. She was taken to a hospital, but later disappeared.

"I thought Dr. Hart was dead," I put in.

"I don't know." Varina glanced at the uneaten pizza on her tray, then looked up to meet our curious gazes.

"Sometimes I have these dreams. Or maybe they're memories."

I nodded, knowing Varina had been cloned with an incredible memory. While I had trouble remembering what happened last week, Varina could recall complete conversations from her infancy.

"So is Jessica Hart in these dreams?" Eric asked Varina, leaning forward in his chair.

"Yes. When I first started having the dreams, I thought she was my guardian angel. She has pretty red hair, a wonderful smile, and she tells me how much she loves me." Varina began tearing small pieces off the napkin in her lap. "But the dream I had last night was different. And I'm beginning to wonder. . . ."

"What?" Eric and I both asked.

"Nothing really." She shrugged and gave a small, shaky laugh. "My dreams are just memories. They can't be actual conversations. Right?"

Eric said "no" at the same time I said "yes."

I shot Eric a "You don't know anything" glance, then said to Varina, "Maybe you're experiencing astral projections. Or you could have a psychic connection with Jessica Hart. All kinds of unexplained things are possible."

"So speaks Miss New Age Allison." Eric rolled his eyes. "I don't think dreams are mysterious."

"You just don't understand them," I retorted.

"There's nothing to understand."

"So speaks Mr. Skeptic."

"Face it, Allison. Dreams are just dreams and they mean absolutely nothing."

"I hope last night's dream meant nothing," Varina admitted, the paper napkin now confetti in her lap. "But it seemed so real. Like I was in the room with Jessica, feeling her hand holding mine and seeing her tears. She warned me of danger."

"Maybe Dr. Hart is communicating beyond the grave," I said. "I've read of ghostly messages like that in magazines. They only happen to sensitive people and shouldn't be ignored. Did Dr. Hart say what kind of danger?"

"No." Varina shrugged. "I woke up suddenly and my heart was pounding. I felt afraid, although I didn't know why."

"Maybe she knows the Victors are going to cause trouble again," I guessed.

Eric regarded us skeptically. "We don't even know for sure *who* called Uncle Jim."

"Too bad Chase isn't here," Varina said wistfully. "He could have told us. With his hearing, he would have heard both sides of Uncle Jim's phone call."

"Yeah. But Chase has enough problems of his own." I envisioned our blond, eighteen-year-old fellow clone. He was in Reno, settling his parents' financial estate. They had died in a fire that was intended to kill him.

"Next time Chase calls, I'll convince him to stay with us. This is where he belongs." Varina gave a dreamy smile. She had a major crush on Chase, but I worried it was one-sided.

"It'd be great if Chase moved in. Then all of us clones would be together like a real family." I leaned forward in my chair, flinching when my bruised hands brushed solid wood, but otherwise feeling fine.

"Except for Sandee Yoon," Eric pointed out. "She doesn't even know she's a clone."

"She had her chance to learn the truth, but she ran away." Varina twirled a strand of her auburn hair around her finger and frowned. "It's Chase I'm concerned about. He was so troubled last time I saw him."

"Troubled about what?" I asked, sensing a secret. Did she know something about Chase we didn't?

"Well . . ." She glanced away. "Being a clone is hard on him."

"It was a shock to all of us," I said.

"But it's different for Chase. I—I can't really explain, but believe me, he has *a lot* to deal with. And I'm worried—" Varina glanced away. "I'm worried he won't ever come back."

"Chase can take care of himself," Eric said. "But I'm not so sure about Uncle Jim."

I nodded. "I hope he doesn't get so stressed he ends up back in the hospital."

"We have to help him." Eric stood up and crumpled his empty paper plate. "I can start by checking the web for information on Jessica Hart. It's worth a try."

"Good idea," I said, remembering it had only taken Eric five minutes to find Cressida Ray's address for me.

"It's a long shot, since Dr. Hart's been missing for over a decade." Eric looked doubtful. "That's a very cold trail even in cyberspace."

"Uncle Jim could tell us if he weren't so stubborn. He's not being fair." Varina balled her ripped napkin in her hand.

"Yeah," I agreed. "He expects us to tell him everything, but he won't tell us anything. We should just go into his office and demand the truth."

"But he was so upset over that call," Varina said uneasily. "This is a bad time to push him."

"Will there ever be a good time?" I countered.

"Probably not," Varina admitted.

"Yeah," Eric agreed. "Let's just do it."

Varina looked at us uncertainly, then nodded. "Okay."

We left the living room. Excitement filled me, and I wondered if we would finally learn more about the cloning experiment. Like who invented the Enhance-X25 formula that gave us super skills? What went wrong with the cloning experiment? And what happened to Jessica Hart?

But as we started down the hall, there was a sudden knock at the front door.

"It's kind of late for visitors," Eric complained.

"I'll get it," I offered, hoping it wasn't Dusty Stiff-Bottom returning.

But when I opened the door, the elegant woman who stood before me definitely wasn't Dustin. She had long wavy blond hair, dark eyes, and a wide smile I'd have recognized anywhere. I'd never met her before, and yet I knew immediately who she was.

Cressida Ray.

My clone.

FIVE

"Allison Beaumont?" Cressida questioned, her voice wavering with nervousness.

Maybe she was nervous, but I was in *total* shock.

My mouth sagged open and I couldn't speak. All I could think was: *My clone. Here!*

I kept staring at this grown-up version of me. She glowed with fragile grace and youthful looks. Her smooth skin was unlined, her wide lips shimmered with peach gloss, and her dark eyes pooled deep.

Was this what I'd look like in another twenty years?

Geez, I didn't look this good now!

She reached out, tentatively, and touched my cheek. "Amazing," she said in a breathy whisper. "You look exactly like I did at your age. The picture you sent was startling."

"You got my letter?" I asked, overjoyed. "You actually read it and came all the way here to see me?"

She nodded, nervously clutching a small amber purse that matched her low-heeled shoes. "I had to see if . . . if you were real."

"I'm real all right." I glanced out to the street, where a long silver limousine was parked by the curb. "Uh, would you like to come inside?"

"How sweet of you to offer. I'll have to check with Dolores first." She turned around and raised her hand in some kind of signal toward the limo. A stocky, gray-haired man wearing a dark suit and white gloves stepped out of the driver's seat and walked around to open a back door for a short pear-shaped woman with dark bobbed hair. The woman stepped out and came toward us.

"Dolores, look at her!" Cressida gestured toward me. "Isn't the resemblance amazing?"

"Absolutely." Dolores's expression was tight and impatient. "But now that you've seen her, we should be going."

"Oh, please, not yet. Would it be okay to go inside for a few minutes?" Cressida asked with a cajoling smile, like a child seeking permission from a parent.

"Of course it's all right. But we do have that shoot with *Fashion Plate Magazine* in the morning, so pace your energy." Dolores carried a dignified briefcase, yet wore casual navy-blue sweats and white sneakers. "I'll come inside with you."

"Sure. Please come in." I glanced at the two women, feeling out of place. "Uh, you'll have to excuse all the boxes. We're still moving in."

"You have a lovely home," Cressida said as she swept into the foyer.

"Oh, I'm boarding here right now with Professor Fergus. My parents live in Seattle."

Varina and Eric stepped forward, both of them clearly curious about my guests. I gestured toward the two women. "This is Cressida Ray and Dolores . . ." I paused, not knowing Dolores's last name.

The short woman extended her hand politely to Eric

and Varina. "I'm Dolores Schwartz, Ms. Ray's manager."

"I wrote a letter to Cressida Ray," I told Varina, knowing it wasn't really an explanation. Varina still looked puzzled; she was probably trying to figure out why I would write to a model. Or maybe she was surprised by Cressida's resemblance to me. But she'd have to wait till later to hear the whole explanation.

The five of us went into the living room.

A large box of Professor Fergus's reference books was blocking the love seat, so I reached down with both hands and gave it a gentle push. *Swoosh!* The box sailed across the room, knocking over a wooden magazine rack.

I grinned sheepishly, reminding myself to control my power. I hurried over and straightened up the magazines. "Sorry. I'm not usually such a klutz." I turned to Cressida with an awed smile. "But it's not every day I meet a famous model. I still can't believe you're here."

"Oh, I'm not famous. Maybe fifteen years ago, but not anymore."

"Rubbish," Dolores snorted. "Your career is on an upswing and the offers are pouring in."

"Just call me the comeback cover model." Cressida shrugged as if joking, then flipped back her hair the same way I did when I was embarrassed by a compliment.

"You look familiar," Varina said with a sharp glance at me.

"She should," Dolores said matter-of-factly. "Cressida might not be a supermodel yet, but she's much sought after for print work and commercials."

"A commercial for hand cream. That's where I've seen her." Varina paused, and then quoted: "Use Comfort cream and age spots will fade away. If *you* don't give your real age away, your hands won't either."

"Wonderful!" Cressida applauded. "Are you an actress?"

"Me?" Varina touched her chest in surprise. "Not even!"

"Varina has an amazing memory," I said.

Cressida turned to me with a smile. "And I'll bet you're amazing, too, Allison. That's why I came here."

"Well . . . I'm glad." I flipped back my braid, not sure what to say. So naturally I rambled on like an idiot. "It's great you're here. I had hoped for a letter or a phone call, but this is even better. Meeting you, I mean."

"I had to come. I couldn't stop thinking about your picture. You know, I've never had any children. But if I'd had a daughter, she'd look like you." Cressida impulsively reached out and clasped my hand.

I looked down and saw our hands together; the same long, slender fingers, although my skin was tanned and hers was pale. Also, her fingernails shone with pearly-pink polish while mine were chipped and stained from outdoor work. Still, there was no doubt in my mind we were duplicates. Carbon copies. Clones.

I wondered how much Cressida knew about my unusual birth. Could the doctors have used her DNA without her knowledge? Was that possible? Or had she volunteered to help with the cloning experiment? But I didn't know how to ask these questions. Not yet, anyway.

Dolores tapped her sneakers against the floor. "Cressida, we should go."

"But I'm not ready yet. I've hardly had any time with Allison." Cressida's full lips puckered in a pout and she narrowed her blond brows—another mannerism I recognized. Except that I'd stopped pulling tantrums when I began to go to boarding school.

"Why don't you come back tomorrow after you finish working," I suggested, ignoring the warning look Eric gave me.

"I'd like that a lot. We could go somewhere and get to know each other." Cressida glanced over at her manager. "Dolores, can we fit it into the schedule?"

"Sorry, but it's not an option. You'll be too exhausted after your photo shoot." Dolores shook her dark head. I decided I did NOT like this bossy little woman.

"No. I won't be tired."

"After the shoot, we check out of the hotel, then fly to Chicago. And Monday morning you've got an interview."

"So *cancel* the flight and the interview."

"Don't be ridiculous. Now come along." Dolores stood and held out her hand to Cressida, a firm signal of who was in charge. "You've satisfied your curiosity. It's time to leave."

"I suppose." Although Cressida stood obediently, I noticed a rebellious gleam in her dark eyes. "First I want to say good-bye to Allison. Please go to the limo and give us a few minutes."

"Of course." Dolores's smile oozed with victory as she turned and left the house.

Cressida and I stood awkwardly for a moment. I smiled shyly at her, while Varina and Eric looked on as if they were watching a dramatic live-action soap opera.

"It worked!" Cressida rubbed her hands together. "Now that she's gone, we can make some plans."

"Plans?" I echoed, puzzled.

"Oh, yes, Allison. Some very exciting plans. I didn't come this far to meet the girl who could be my twin and not have a chance to get to know her." She flashed a mischievous grin and declared, "So this is what we're going to do. . . ."

SIX

I could hardly sleep that night. Ideas, worries, and excitement ricocheted through my head like rapidly fired pinballs. Would Cressida's plan work? Could she trust her limo driver to help? What if her manager guessed something was up? And even if the plan did work, how long before someone found us?

Tucking my pillow snugly under my head, I stretched out on my back and stared upward. The moon's glow from my window caused silvery rays to shift on the ceiling. My thoughts shifted with them; from Cressida to Professor Fergus to fear.

That phone call. He'd been so frightened, traumatized, his distress clearly not for himself but for Jessica. Had he loved Dr. Hart? Was that one of the secrets he kept from us?

After Cressida left, while Eric headed for the backyard to feed the yellow dog Renegade, Varina and I had gone to Professor Fergus's office and knocked on the door.

"Uncle Jim, please open up," Varina had called. "You have to tell us what's going on. We're worried about you."

But her uncle hadn't answered. Varina said he might be sleeping, so we'd left.

In a way I was relieved. I knew I'd have to tell him about the construction accident and about meeting Cressida. But I was afraid of his reaction and didn't mind putting off the discussion. Besides, he might not approve of my spending time with the woman I was cloned from. He was so secretive about the cloning experiment, hinting at unknown dangers and warning us to tell no one about our true pasts. There was a good chance he'd forbid me to see Cressida again—which was something I just couldn't bear.

Cressida had been *so* great. Her quick smile invited friendship and her hand-squeeze warmed my heart. She'd even come up with a plan so we could steal a few hours together. She seemed as fascinated with me as I was with her. And I sensed her interest went beyond my looks, that she had a keen desire to get to know me— as if she guessed or knew we had more than coincidence in common.

The moon disappeared under heavy clouds and the ceiling shadows blended to darkness. My thoughts dipped deeper toward dreams, and as I fell asleep I pondered the most important question of all.

Did Cressida know I was her clone?

SEVEN

At ten o'clock Sunday morning, shortly after Professor Fergus drove Eric to church, I heard two sharp honks from outside.

"The car's here!" I exclaimed, dancing away from the large front window and racing for my purse. I snatched it off the kitchen counter and hurried to the front door.

Varina met me there with a solemn gaze. "I hope you know what you're doing."

"I haven't a clue." I laughed, my long braid flipping behind me. "And I don't care. This is so exciting. A secret meeting with a new friend."

"She's more than your *friend*," Varina accused.

"Yeah, I know." I gulped. "Did Eric tell you?"

"He didn't have to. Anyone can see how much you look alike. How did you find her?"

"I saw her picture on an old magazine. Then Eric tracked down her address on the web."

"And you wrote to her. You probably sent her a picture, too."

"It worked, didn't it? I found her."

"And now she's found you." Varina pushed back her auburn bangs and said quietly, "Uncle Jim isn't going to like this."

"Then don't tell him. It's not like I'm going to blab to Cressida about being her clone. I don't think she knows. Besides, she's only going to be in town for one more day. Afterward, I may never see her again."

"Or maybe we'll never see *you* again," Varina said ominously. "What if she's working with the Victors? Maybe this is all a scam to kidnap you."

"That's crazy!" I shook my head incredulously. "I'm the one who wrote to *her*. Being with her won't be dangerous to anyone. I promise I'll be very careful."

"Take your cell phone so you can call if you have trouble."

"Yes, Mother."

"Don't joke. I have a bad feeling about this. Hanging out with the woman you were cloned from is risky— especially a model who's famous. Someone might see you together and guess your secret."

"Lots of people look alike."

"But most people don't have a clone. It was a shock to see you and Cressida side by side. You look, move, and sound alike."

"Yeah. Isn't it the coolest?" I asked with delight. "You of all people should understand, Varina. You have a clone somewhere, too. Don't you want to meet her?"

Varina bit her lip and glanced away. She paused and then said softly, "Maybe I already *have* met her."

"What do you mean?"

"Nothing for sure. Just a dim memory." She shook her head. "Uncle Jim's the only one who can tell me if . . . if my suspicions are true."

"I don't need anyone to tell me about my DNA donor. I've found her and we're going to be great friends. Biologically she's closer to me than anyone in the world. It's like she *is* me."

"No, Allison. You're your own person. Maybe you share DNA with Cressida, but you've lived very different lives."

"Oh, I know! She's actually *lived* her life, while I haven't even begun to figure out mine. I can learn a lot from her." I heard a honk from outside and opened the door. "Gotta go!"

"I still think it's a bad idea, but have fun anyway." Varina reached out to give me a hug. "And be careful."

"Oh, I will!" Then I practically flew out of the house, down the steps, and toward the waiting car. Not just any car, either—an awesome silver stretch limo! The most elaborate one I'd ever seen. Wow! This was going to be the most thrilling day of my entire life.

EIGHT

Chauffeur Leo opened the door for me. I slipped grace-fully into the backseat. I hadn't been in a limo since I was a little girl, back when it was a thrill to attend political events with my parents. They'd sandwich me between them, each holding one of my hands, and proudly show me off. I still had some newspaper clip-pings of that cute little blond girl who smiled and looked like a dress-up doll in ruffles and silk.

How disappointing for my parents when I'd switched from silk to denim. They'd gone to such extremes to adopt a baby, but I guess they'd forgotten babies even-tually grow up.

Yet sitting in the back of the plush limo, I didn't feel grown-up. I felt like a little kid headed for Disneyland. Soft music played from compact speakers and I glanced curiously at the many buttons and gadgets surrounding the leather seats. There was a TV, a laptop, a cell phone, and even a small refrigerator.

"Help yourself to something to drink," the chauffeur said, his voice gruff but not unfriendly. The dark glass partition that separated us was down a few inches and I could see his glove on the steering wheel as he drove off.

"Thanks." I opened the refrigerator and found a wide selection of soft drinks, flavored water, juices, wine, and assorted snacks. I decided on a bottle of kiwi-peach water.

As I sipped, I stared out the window, enjoying the bold stares and curious glances a limo attracts. It was nice to realize no one could see inside the tinted glass. I was protected like a princess inside her royal carriage.

"Where are we headed?" I called out to the driver when he stopped for a red light.

"Fountain Plaza." The light turned green and he hit the gas. "It's only a few blocks away."

"Yeah. I've been there before." I had a quick image of the ultramodern plaza with elegant boutiques and specialty shops.

"Miss Ray should be finishing her shoot shortly."

"Will I be able to watch?"

"If you're careful to keep out of sight."

"I will," I assured him.

The limo made a left turn, then pulled into the vast parking lot of Fountain Plaza. It was still early, so the stores weren't open yet. But there was a flurry of activity: people, cars, and even a portable trailer by the mall entrance where a huge fountain spurted dancing colored waterfalls.

And there was Cressida. Artificial lights caused her gold and ebony swimsuit to glow, setting her loose blond hair aflame. She moved quickly; practiced turns, twists, smiles, pouts, head tosses, and laughter, the camera capturing her magic perfectly.

"Stay here," the driver cautioned as we slowed beside one of the trailers.

"Okay." But I was disappointed, because the trailer partly blocked my view and I couldn't clearly see what was going on. I twisted around to peer through the back window, and was rewarded by a glimpse of Cressida. I pushed a button and rolled the window down a crack. Voices drifted in, and I heard someone shout, "It's a wrap!"

Excitement leaped within me.

Now the *real* fun would begin!

With my face pressed against the window, I watched as Cressida dabbed her brow with a towel and then waved to a few people. Dolores and a tall, lanky man wearing a dignified business suit approached her. The tall man spoke to Cressida, his sharp face tensed with anger.

"Who is that man?" I asked, catching the driver's attention in the rearview mirror.

"Jackson Goodwin. Miss Ray's agent. Of course, he used to be her husband, too. Thankfully, that's over." Then Leo shrugged and pointed in a different direction. "See that skinny redhead sitting on the grass over there? That's Sarah Ann. She's Miss Ray's stepdaughter. Thinks she's a model like Miss Ray. Humph!"

I could tell by his gruff tone that he didn't share Sarah Ann's opinion. But why couldn't Sarah Ann be a model? She was slender and very cute, older than me but shorter, with kinky red hair that reminded me of Little Orphan Annie. I bet Cressida was proud Sarah Ann wanted to follow in her modeling footsteps. Although it seemed odd for my DNA double to have a grown stepdaughter.

Cressida's ex-husband/agent said something angrily that I couldn't hear. She shook her head and argued back, which caused Mr. Goodwin to stomp his foot and storm off. I didn't have time to wonder about this, because Cressida was on the move.

"She's coming this way!" I exclaimed as I squirmed in my seat. "But Dolores and Sarah Ann are with her. They'll ruin everything."

"Patience. Miss Ray knows what she's doing," the

chauffeur assured me with the confidence of a proud father. "Behind her sweet smile is one smart lady."

Cressida kept walking toward the limo. Sarah Ann said something I couldn't hear, then stopped suddenly and headed back toward the camera crew. Unfortunately, Dolores didn't leave. She remained with Cressida, holding some papers and talking as she hurried along.

They neared the limo, and I held my breath and waited.

I could see Cressida clearly now, and noticed the little pucker of worry on her forehead as she tossed a helpless glance in my direction. Of course, she couldn't see me through the tinted glass, but she knew I was here.

The window was still open a crack and I could hear Dolores talking about important papers that needed to be signed. But Cressida shook her head. "It's always business first with you and Jackson. But I need to change out of these clothes. It'll just be a minute," I heard her say. Then she slipped into the trailer.

"Now what? Why did she go in there?" I murmured. But the driver had shut the window that separated us.

I waited anxiously, tapping my fingers on the leather seats, glancing up every other second, watching the front of the trailer and wondering when Cressida would come out.

Dolores also waited, her expression tense. She sat down on a wooden bench, shifting uncomfortably and shuffling the papers in her lap.

After a few minutes, I glimpsed movement from the back of the trailer. A window was opening. And a blond head wearing a dark cap peeked out. It was Cressida! She crawled through the window; first her feet, then legs, and *whoosh*!

She jumped to the ground, wearing snug black jeans and a loose yellow T-shirt with a dark windbreaker. She ducked low and glanced around cautiously as she hurried toward us.

Then Cressida was scooting inside the limo, laughing and full of delight as she exclaimed, *"I did it!"*

"You sure did." I laughed with her, and we were still laughing when the chauffeur started the limo up.

I gave one last glance to the front of the trailer, where Dolores was still waiting. With her arms crossed impatiently, she frowned at her watch and tapped her foot.

She's going to have a long wait.

Cressida took my hand. "My plan worked!" she said enthusiastically.

"It sure did. You're free of that bossy Dolores."

"As well as Jackson and everyone else who insists on running my life. I'm going to enjoy my freedom by having fun. With you. Ready to be adventurous?"

"What do you mean?"

"Ah! That's my surprise. You'll never guess where we're going!"

NINE

Where would a sophisticated model go for fun?

I puzzled over this as the limousine drove on.

"Are we going to a movie?" I asked Cressida, enjoying the low rocking sounds of Ravage on the stereo. I opened another bottle of flavored water. This time I chose strawberry lime.

"No. Not a movie." Cressida smiled and took a sip of her diet soda.

I thought of the places Mother used to take me when I was younger. "An art gallery? A museum? An observatory?"

Cressida shook her head, pulling off her concealing cap so that her blond hair spilled around her slender shoulders. Even in jeans and a T-shirt, she looked glamorous.

The limo turned right, away from bustling traffic and toward a quieter industrial area where large warehouses stretched to the sky. I didn't know this area well, and my curiosity peaked.

"Where *are* we headed?"

Cressida pursed her lips mysteriously and shook her head. "You'll find out. Besides, I'd rather hear about *you*. I'm still astonished by how much you look like me. You even have a mole on your neck in the same place I do. Unbelievable!"

"It's not really so unbelievable," I said cautiously. "I was adopted, so maybe we're related."

"I doubt it." She set her soda on a table and smiled gently. "I've never had any children of my own. My younger sister isn't married yet and my brothers all have very young children. We have huge family reunions every year, so I'd know if we were related."

"Maybe I'm a distant relative."

"I suppose it's possible. Do you know anything about your biological parents?"

Change that to *parent*, singular, I thought wryly. I took a deep breath, debating on whether to tell her the truth.

I wanted her to know, and yet I'd promised Professor Fergus not to tell anyone. But Cressida wasn't just *anyone*. She was like me. Still, I didn't know her well enough to reveal such an important secret. Not yet, anyway.

"Miss Ray, sorry to interrupt." The tinted window separating us from the driver had lowered a few inches. "But we have a problem."

"What?" Cressida glanced up, instantly on edge.

"Look behind us. That green van," he said ominously. "Looks like Dominique."

"Dominique?" I questioned, turning around in my seat. Sure enough, there was a green van, its solitary driver obscured by shadows.

"Dominique! Not again!" Cressida slapped her hand on her lap. "I thought I'd left her in Los Angeles. Won't she ever give up?"

"Who is she?" I wanted to know.

"A pest." Cressida frowned as we made another turn and the green van followed.

My fingers tightened around my strawberry drink. "What's going on?"

"Nothing to worry about, just an inconvenience." She spoke lightly, and yet I knew my own reactions too well not to recognize the worry in her gaze. "Dominique Eszlinger—or as I call her, 'the Mudslinger'—writes lies for a scandal sheet called *EXPOSED!*"

"Oh, I've seen that magazine. It has wild stories, like Elvis being reincarnated or a fashion show for overweight aliens." I usually enjoyed reading bizarre articles, but *EXPOSED!* was way too outrageous. Even their weather forecasts were fiction.

What if Dominique had found out I was Cressida's clone?

"Hang on tight!" the driver called out, and suddenly the car jerked around, tires screeching as we made a sharp U-turn. Strawberry-lime sloshed from my bottle, sprinkling my face. Yuck!

"Here's a napkin," Cressida offered, her drink securely in her hand and not a drop of liquid sloshed on her clothes. "We can count on Leo. He's been with me for twenty years, and he's a fantastic driver."

"Why is he so stiff?" I asked with a curious glance to the front seat. The separating window was still open a crack, so I kept my voice low.

"Leo is a bit formal, probably because of his military background, but he's like a father to me. I'd trust him with my life, and you can, too." Cressida turned to look out the window, and then smiled. "See! The van is gone!"

I looked behind us. No sign of the van. Major relief! The last thing I needed was to have my clone past exposed by *EXPOSED!*

A few blocks later, the limo slowed in front of a large gray industrial building.

"Here we are!" Cressida rang out. "Let the adventure begin."

"Adventure? In a warehouse?"

"Look closer." She pointed to a small sign in the front corner of the building that read: Rock Climbing Castle, The Ultimate Indoor Climbing Experience.

"Wow!" I murmured. Cressida hadn't been kidding about wanting an adventure. I'd never been rock climbing before, but hey, it sounded cool.

There was no doubt about it: Cressida was definitely me all grown up: impulsive, living in the moment, with an outrageous sense of fun. Physically, though, she seemed fragile. Too bad she hadn't been born with the Enhance-X25 formula that gave me extra strength. I hoped rock climbing wasn't too strenuous for her.

Together, we left the limo and headed for the building. Cressida giggled, slipping her arm around me like we were longtime girlfriends or close family. A strong yearning hit me. If only Cressida and I *were* family; sisters, or even better, mother and daughter.

"I've always wanted to try one of these places. This is going to be so thrilling," Cressida said as she opened her purse and handed several bills to an attendant. In return, we were given a pair of squishy, worn, dirt-ugly climbing shoes. And while it was a surprise to Cressida that we wore the exact same narrow size, it was no surprise to me.

I'd never seen an indoor rock climbing place before, and was duly impressed by the awesome gray stone castle design. A maze of fabricated walls towered throughout the sprawling building. Most walls stood straight like saluting soldiers, but others leaned at awkward angles; tilting, curving, and winding.

All the walls had specially created handholds, some molded into half-moons, shamrocks, and hearts. There were even challenging handholds across the top of the ceiling. One brave soul dangled upside down in a topsy-turvy position, his belay rope held firm by a buddy.

We followed an instructor named Rebekah to a gently sloping wall, the equivalent of a "bunny slope" at a ski resort. Rebekah teased that we must be twins, which caused Cressida to beam but made me uneasy. I couldn't risk being noticed. Anxiously, I glanced around, but no one else seemed interested in us.

Rebekah gave us quick lessons, showing us how to use our feet to push off the wall in a sitting position with the belay rope holding us in midair. She told us to place our feet on the protruding rocks and to reach up for a firm handhold.

It looked easy enough once Rebekah helped fasten the belay harness correctly around my waist. Cressida urged me to go first, and I didn't hesitate. The attendant held my safety rope and I scrambled up like a monkey, reaching the top in less than a minute.

"Hey, that was fun!" I called down, kicking off the wall and gliding downward. "Your turn now."

"You bet!" Cressida replied, already clipping the belay rope to her harness and reaching for one of the heart-shaped rocks. But her legs sprawled awkwardly and her fingers slipped. When she swung upward and grabbed another rocky handhold, her feet dangled like two floppy worms on a fishhook.

"I—I can do this." Cressida gritted her teeth with determination. Then she tried again, climbing several feet off the ground. She clung tight to the handhold and reached higher. Her legs trembled, her lips were tinged blue, and her breathing grew heavy. The climb was taking a toll on her energy.

"Maybe you should come down," I said, sensing that something wasn't right.

"No." She puffed hard. "I—I can do·. . . do it."

I wasn't so sure, and could tell that the instructor was growing anxious, too. But Cressida continued climbing, her skin paper-white and her breathing increasingly ragged.

Just as she reached the top, someone shrieked, "Cressida! What in heaven's name are you doing?"

Startled, Cressida lost her grip. She slipped and fell, her arms flailing. But she didn't fall far; the safety harness held her firmly. With a choked gasp, she swayed back and forth in midair.

I whirled around and saw Dolores running toward us. Her expression was both angry and horrified. What was she doing here? And she wasn't alone. Hurrying beside her were Cressida's ex-husband/agent Jackson and his daughter Sarah Ann.

Dolores grabbed my arm roughly. "How could you?" she demanded. "Are you trying to kill her?"

"Of course not!" The accusation shocked me, and I felt my mouth fall open. "I—I . . . We were just having fun."

"That kind of fun will send Cressida to a hospital." Dolores glared at me, then released my arm and rushed over to help Cressida out of the belay harness.

"Is she all right?" Jackson asked, his gaze full of concern and worry.

"Of course she's all right. She was just climbing a wall, not Mount Everest," I said sarcastically. "You guys are totally overreacting."

"We probably saved her life," snapped Dolores.

"What are you talking about?" I scrunched my forehead. "Climbing isn't dangerous."

"Maybe not for most people," the ex-husband said. "But Cressy has never been like most people." He suddenly blinked and stared at me in amazement. Then he glanced back at Cressida before returning his gaze to me.

Instead of speaking to me, he went over to Dolores, who was at Cressida's side. "Why didn't you tell me?" I heard him say. "She's the image of Cressy!"

"It wasn't important," the manager retorted, then her expression softened as she turned back to Cressida.

I felt a nudge on my shoulder and found Sarah Ann staring at me. "You do look like Cressida," she told me, running her fingers through her curly short red hair. "Who are you?"

"Allison Beaumont. And you're Sarah Ann."

"Yep. Number one stepdaughter." She grinned. "So what's the deal with you and Stepmommy Dearest?"

"I only met Cressida yesterday."

"Yeah, right." Her hazel eyes flickered with skepticism. "Aren't you kind of young to be one of her freaky fans? Did you have plastic surgery so you'd look like her?"

"No way! It's just a coincidence."

"You even *sound* like her." It was an accusation. "No wonder she ran off with you. I bet you even want to be a model. Like everyone in the world."

"No." I shook my head, glancing over to where Cressida was speaking in a quiet, angry tone to her manager and agent. I returned my attention to Sarah Ann and replied firmly, "I definitely do not want to be a model. I like to work outside, building stuff. I hardly even wear makeup."

Sarah Ann knitted her brows. "With a face like Cressida's, you don't need makeup. I have so many freckles, it takes a whole bottle of concealer to tone them down. My mom took me to get a face peel, but that didn't even help. So if you aren't into modeling, why are you hanging out with Cressida?"

"She invited me." It was the truth, but Sarah Ann still looked puzzled.

"Are you related to her? I heard she had a niece, but I thought she was just a little kid."

I didn't know what to say, so it was a relief when I glanced around and saw the others walking our way.

Cressida's shoulders sagged and her expression was solemn.

"Sorry, Allison," she said quietly, "but we have to leave."

"Are you all right?" Her face was awfully pale, and her lips still had a bluish tinge.

"I'm fine, just tired." She glanced uneasily at her manager and agent, who stood like palace guards on each side of her. "I'm sorry we couldn't stay longer."

"Hey, we had fun for a while."

"We sure did. And I even made it to the top," Cressida said proudly.

"You did great." I forced a cheery smile. "Maybe we can go out again next time you're in town."

Dolores made a "humph!" sound, as if that wouldn't happen anytime soon.

Cressida reached out and squeezed my hand, yet the faint smile she offered didn't reach her eyes. Something was wrong. But what? Why did she let these people push her around? She was the successful model; they were only her employees.

With a sigh, I returned the rental shoes and went to find my own. But when I looked under the bench where I'd left them, they were gone.

"Just what I don't need," I grumbled, bending down to search the floor. But my shoes were nowhere to be found. And they were my favorite canvas ankle-boots.

I walked over to the other benches and checked them, too. Still nothing. But when I happened to glance out the large front window, I was stunned to see one of my shoes perched on top of a fence post.

Suspiciously, I glanced around at some children giggling in a corner as they laced up their rock climbing shoes. Were they responsible? Was this their idea of a practical joke?

Frowning, I yanked open the front door and strode outside. I lifted my shoe off the fence post, then looked around for its mate. I didn't see it, but in the parking lot I spotted Cressida stepping into the limousine. She waved, gesturing for me to hurry. I pointed to my feet and the single shoe, then yelled out I'd only be a few more minutes.

I was tempted to go back inside and throttle those bratty kids. If I didn't find my shoe soon, I'd have to leave without it. But clearly it wasn't anywhere near the front of the building. So I walked around to the side, a barren expanse of rocky dirt, stacked boxes, and stinky garbage bins.

Just as I was ready to give up, I saw my shoe.

It was far back by a chain fence on top of a large stack of flattened boxes. Star thistles and weeds snagged my socks as I carefully made my way across the desolate field. In the distance, I heard a car honk and hoped Cressida wouldn't leave without me.

Almost there, I thought as I stepped around some broken glass. This empty area would probably be covered by a building someday, but now it was simply a wasteland.

Stopping at the edge of the flattened boxes, I reached for my shoe. But it was too high. Cautiously, I stepped on the cardboard, then reached again. I still wasn't close enough. So I took another step up the cardboard pile, extending my arm as far as possible. This time my fingers snagged the shoelace. *Yes!*

I gave the lace a firm yank—and my feet wobbled.

I heard the sound of something cracking, and the cardboard beneath me shifted, crumpled, and collapsed. I screamed, flailing my arms. There was nothing to grab on to as the ground sucked me in. I fell down . . . down . . . down—until I crashed with a *thud* into darkness.

TEN

As I woke, my head throbbed, my body ached, and I had no idea how much time had passed since the fall.

Icy cold seeped into my skin, and I shivered. I tried to calm myself with slow breathing. But when I inhaled, the rank odor of damp earth nearly made me gag.

Where was I?

I heard the soft crunch of crumpled cardboard beneath my feet. When I reached out, I realized that my dirt prison was narrow and round, perhaps the remains of an old well. But I couldn't see anything. When I looked up, down, around, there was no light. I felt the shoes I still clutched in my hands, yet couldn't see them in the darkness.

What kind of horrible pit had I fallen into? And why hadn't anyone come to rescue me? Cressida had to realize I was missing by now. So where was she?

Panic struck. I began to scream. "HELP!! HELP!!! SOMEONE GET ME OUT OF HERE!"

I yelled for minutes that seemed like hours. Over and over, punctuated by scream after scream, I pounded my fists against solid dirt walls. But my cries only resulted in eerie echoes.

I was all alone.

In the dark.

Trapped.

Now what? *How was I going to escape?* I sank to the ground and buried my face in my hands. Wet tears dribbled down, warm on my palms. My shivering grew worse.

I couldn't understand why Cressida hadn't come to help. She wouldn't abandon me. *Would she?*

Of course not! We were kindred souls. I shared her DNA, and no way would *I* ever abandon a friend. But Cressida had seemed awfully pale and weak. Maybe she wasn't physically able to come after me. Or worse—what if she was in trouble, too?

This new worry kicked some fight back into me. I couldn't count on help from outside, so I'd have to help myself. *But how?* I wondered as I awkwardly fumbled with my shoes, slipping them on by touch, and even managing to tie them.

Think, Allison! an inner voice urged. *Don't go all soft and wimpy. Stand tall and figure a way out.*

Well, the only way out was up. So that's where I'd go. But how far would I have to climb? Inches, feet, or miles? Still, if climbing was the only way out, I knew I'd better get moving.

So I did.

This dark climb lacked the assistance of fabricated handholds and a belay rope. Finding firm holds on the rough dirt wall wasn't easy. But I couldn't give up.

My arms stretched high and I fumbled around for something solid to grab. Dirt crumbled. My fingers slipped. I tried again, grasping a jutting rock, using my strength to pull myself high, gripping a dangling root next, then another rock, until my head bumped something solid.

I'd reached the top!

But a heavy obstruction blocked the opening. Feeling the rough, hard object, I realized it was a concrete slab, like a cork bottling me alive inside the dirt hole. How had the concrete gotten there? Heavy slabs didn't just appear.

Someone had covered the hole.

Trapping me inside.

On purpose.

ELEVEN

I fought the urge to cry hysterically and curl up in this dirt coffin.

I wouldn't give up, though. I was too impatient for that nonsense. Besides, I was made of sterner stuff: Enhance-X25 formula to be exact. Still, I felt a stab of worry.

Powers, don't fail me now!

I braced myself and pushed up on the heavy block. The weighty slab was as light as a pebble to my touch. There was a horrendous scraping sound and showers of dirt splattered as the concrete slid off.

I blinked tears of relief into bright daylight. Wiping the tears away, I looked down at myself. What a mess! My hands were bruised and scraped beneath a thick layer of dirt. My clothes were covered in dirt, too. And I could only imagine what my face must look like.

But I was alive. And I was free! Thank God!

I left the deserted field. As I hurried around the corner, I was delighted to find the silver limo waiting in the parking lot. I knew I could count on Cressida.

And there she was, hurrying over when she saw me. She waved and jumped excitedly.

"Allison! What happened to you? How'd you get so dirty?"

"I fell," I answered with a small shiver.

"Are you okay? I was so worried!" She wrapped her arms around me, holding tight.

"I'm too dirty to touch." I pushed back, embarrassed by the filth that had rubbed off on her clothes. "I—I had an accident. Or something."

"You poor baby! We looked everywhere for you! I was ready to call the police." She was leading me to the limo, not seeming to mind my filth. "What happened?"

"I fell into a hole." I spoke slowly, confusion sinking in and challenging my thoughts. What *had* happened? Maybe it had been an accident. But then how could I explain the concrete slab? And if I told her about the slab, how could I explain being strong enough to push it away from the hole?

"How did that happen? Are you all right?"

I wasn't the brave silent type, but Cressida looked more pale than ever and I didn't want to worry her. So I forced a small smile and told her it was just a freak accident. "I'm okay now. I just want to go home and soak in a steamy hot bath."

"Are you sure?" she asked with gentle concern as she led me toward the limo.

"Yeah. A little dirt never killed anyone."

"As long as you're safe. It was scary when I couldn't find you. And can you believe Dolores and Jackson wouldn't even help search? I usually trust their judgment, but their attitude really ticked me off. I told them to go back to the hotel."

"You did?" I asked, deeply touched.

"Yeah. I probably shouldn't have lost my temper, but they wouldn't take my worries seriously. Dolores had the nerve to say you probably took off with some friends, and Jackson agreed with her. But I knew you wouldn't leave without letting me know."

"How could you be sure?" I met her gaze in a challenging manner, wondering if she suspected the truth about my birth. "You only met me last night. Maybe I'm a total flake."

"If you're a flake, then you're a loyal one." She gave a small laugh. "Like me."

"Yeah. Like you. A lot like you."

We'd reached the limo, and the chauffeur stepped out to open the back door for us. He didn't ask any questions, but his curious gaze lingered on me. Then he reached into a back compartment and offered me a first aid kit and a towel. The light blue towel had dark smudges on it, as if he used it for dusting chrome or wiping windshields. Regardless, I was grateful for it, although I wondered if Leo was being compassionate or if he simply didn't want me dirtying up his limousine.

After wiping my hands, face, and clothes, I leaned back in the seat, feeling a sense of déjà vu. Yesterday I'd had an accident, and today I'd survived another one. Had I turned into a total klutz, or were these more than coincidences? And did they have anything to do with the Victors and the cloning experiment?

The phone call Professor Fergus received last night from Dr. Victor had disturbed the Professor so badly he still hadn't come out of his room this morning. I had no idea what Dr. Victor had threatened, but it must have been horrible. The guy was a total psycho. In his twisted logic, the only way to repair the ill-fated clone experiment was to terminate the results: Varina, Eric, Chase, Sandee, and me.

Or maybe Geneva Victor was trying to capture a clone again so she could treat us like lab rats. But would she leave the comfort of her wealthy lifestyle to toss a bundle of shakes on me or play hide-and-seek with my shoes? Besides, Dustin had said the person he'd seen on

the roof was a man, not a woman. Had she hired someone to harm me?

I didn't know what to think, and I was afraid.

"I'm sorry today didn't turn out like I planned," Cressida said as the car took off.

"It wasn't your fault."

"Maybe not directly, but I shouldn't have left the
Rock Climbing Castle brochure in my trailer. That's
how Dolores found us." Her half-smile held sadness and
regret.

"Well I had a great time rock climbing, even if it was
short." I gave her a deep look. "But I don't understand
why you let your manager run your life. Doesn't Dolores
work for you?"

"Yes, but it's more complicated than that." Her gaze
strayed out the window, her loose blond hair slipping
over one side of her face. When she turned back to me
I saw uncertainty in her dark eyes. "You see, I owe
Dolores so much."

"So she's a good manager and helped your career.
That doesn't mean you have to do what she says."

"She's only watching out for me. She doesn't want
me to get hurt."

"Rock climbing won't hurt you."

"I know that, but Dolores worries, for a good reason."
Cressida's lower lip trembled, and she added, "Maybe I
should tell you my secret."

Secret? The word made my heart jump and ping-pong
with expectations. Maybe she *did* know about the cloning experiment.

But my guess was wrong.

What Cressida revealed had *nothing* to do with me.

TWELVE

The limousine slowed, tangled in traffic due to a construction zone, and I had to lean forward to hear Cressida's whispered revelation.

"I don't want Leo to hear this. He's like a dear father, and he'd only worry," she confessed. "It's bad enough Dolores knows, but she's my manager, so that can't be helped."

"What is it?"

"Last year, I nearly died."

"Died?" I gave a soft gasp. "How?"

She lifted her hand and placed it on her chest. "I have a weak heart. I always have."

"What do you mean?"

"I was born with a damaged heart. The doctors didn't think I would live long, but I proved them wrong. And up until a year ago, except for bouts of tiredness, I'd lived a normal life." She took a deep breath, her lips showing a hint of blue despite her orange lip gloss. "Only last year, while filming a commercial where I had to run along the beach, I passed out."

"No!"

She nodded grimly. "When I woke up, I was in the hospital. And later I found out that my heart had worsened. They warned me that if I didn't take it easy, my heart would fail completely. So I've been taking it easy . . . most of the time." Her mouth twisted with humor. "Except today. I just wanted to let go and have fun. Can you understand?"

"Sure." I crossed my legs, shifted in my seat, weighing my next words. "But you look so good, not sick or anything. It's hard to believe you almost died."

"Believe it." She blew out a heavy breath. "I'm only glad Jackson and Dolores have been able to keep it from the media. Can you imagine if Dominique the Mudslinger found out I was one step away from an organ donor list? She'd blast it all over her sleazy magazine!"

"And yet you told me," I said with awe and growing affection. "That means a lot. And I promise not to breathe a word of your secret to anyone."

"Thanks." She reached out and squeezed my hand. "You're a special girl, Allison. I've never met anyone quite like you."

"Oh, yes you have," I replied, unable to resist a smile.

"Don't be modest. Despite the problems, today has meant a lot to me. I wish I didn't have to leave so soon."

"Yeah. Maybe we could go sky diving or bungee jumping." I saw her horrified expression, then laughed and quickly added, "Just teasing. But I wasn't teasing about wanting you to stay longer."

We were both quiet as the limousine slowed and turned onto my street. Good-byes were hard, but I managed to smile and hide my sadness. Though she promised we'd see each other again, I knew it wouldn't happen. She was too busy being "Cressida" and I had school tomorrow.

Then the limousine zoomed off down the street, taking my soul mate away and out of my life.

"Okay. Back to reality," I told myself firmly as I walked into my home. I thought about how I'd spend the rest of the evening. There was that algebra assignment, a favorite TV show, and I still hadn't read my latest *Hard Hat Digest* magazine. But first I'd soak in a luxurious hot bath with strawberry bath oil and honey-rose body lotion. Then I'd tell my friends about my near-death experience.

When I stepped inside the foyer and glanced around, I sensed that something had changed. Peeking inside the living room, I found it deserted, and yet improved. The moving boxes were gone, replaced with artfully arranged furniture, bookshelves, framed paintings, and other homey touches. Walking down the hall, I noticed more wall paintings, as well as some Fergus family portraits. Someone had been very busy while I was away today.

"Hey, I'm home!" I called out, noticing that the door to Professor Fergus's office was closed, as was the door to the adjoining bedroom. But the bedroom across the hall, which was going to be for guests, was open. And a glance inside showed a brown suitcase and a few boxes scattered across the green chenille bedspread.

"Anyone here?" I called again. This time I heard a muffled reply, and then the door to Professor Fergus's office burst open.

"It's about time, Allison," Eric said, his dark hand pressed lightly against the door. He did a double take and stared at me. "Allison! What happened? You look like you just lost a mud-wrestling contest."

"Close. But luckily I didn't lose."

"You're okay, aren't you?"

"Nothing a hot bath won't fix." I glanced into the room and saw three familiar faces sitting in chairs around Professor Fergus's desk: Varina, her uncle, and Chase.

Chase Rinaldi was here!

Overjoyed, I squealed his name and rushed over to

him. He'd always been a bit on the dark and moody side; distraught over losing his parents and discovering he was a clone. But I was thrilled he was here. It had been months since I'd last seen him.

"When did you get here?" I started to hug him, but then pulled back when I remembered that my clothes were dirt-splattered. Instead, I jumped excitedly. "Why didn't you tell us you were coming? Does this mean you're moving in? Wow! I'm so thrilled you're here!"

Chase laughed, and smoothed back a strand of his blond hair. "I'm cool about being here, too. You sure know how to make a guy welcome, Al. But, hey, what happened to you?"

Varina gave me a concerned look. "How'd you get so dirty?"

"I fell into a hole."

"That must have been some hole," Chase murmured with a whistle. "What happened?"

"It's a long story and before I tell it, I really need a hot bath. I'm totally beat." I pushed back my hair, and saw specks of dirt fall from my head. Geez, I really was a mess! That bath was sounding better by the minute.

But Professor Fergus, who had been quietly listening until now, cleared his throat. He tapped the eraser end of a pencil on his desk, and looked at me. "Allison, I apologize for being so distracted. And I'm eager to hear about your day, but the reason we're all gathered here— the reason Chase made a trip from Reno to join us—is more pressing."

His tone was ominous, and I tensed. "What reason?"

Varina laid a comforting hand on her uncle's shoulder and told us, "It's about that phone call yesterday."

"Yes." Professor Fergus rubbed his wrinkled forehead. "You may have guessed the call was from my former associate, Dr. Victor."

"The murderer," Chase said bitterly.

Professor Fergus nodded, four sets of eyes fixed on

him. And the room grew quiet, except for a dark-wood grandfather clock in the corner that ticked rhythmically.

"As you know, I feel responsible for each of you," Professor Fergus began. "And I'm honored to have you living with me. But I know your lives haven't been easy. And that blame lies heavy on me."

"You've done your best," Varina assured, touching his arm.

"It hasn't been enough." He gave a low sigh. "Since the experiment, I've learned to value the human aspect of science. You kids have helped teach me. Still, my concern for your safety has kept me from being completely honest with you."

"What do you mean?" Varina asked.

"I thought ignoring the past would protect everyone involved. But not so." His shoulders sagged and his graying brows knit together. "Someone I care for deeply may be in danger, and I don't even know how to find her. So I'm turning to you kids."

"We'll be glad to help," Eric offered.

"Darned straight," Chase added.

Varina and I nodded our support, too.

"Thanks." Professor Fergus's smile was faint. "But first you need to know the truth. That's why I've decided to tell you what really happened almost twenty years ago, when three doctors decided to create human clones. . . ."

THIRTEEN

I clasped my hands together, hooked them around my knees, and leaned forward in my chair. Since discovering I was a clone, I'd been dying to know the real facts behind my birth. Now my curiosity was so intense I could barely contain myself.

"Before things turned for the worse, Dr. Victor, Dr. Hart, and I were colleagues in a biology lab," Professor Fergus began in a grave tone. "We were hired to analyze and report on ways to improve agricultural crops. My pet project was a new strain of spinach."

"Spinach?" Varina repeated with distaste. "Yuck!"

"I happen to like vegetables," I put in proudly.

Professor Fergus gave a wry smile. "At first it was very exciting. Especially when Dr. Hart developed the Enhance-X25 formula. Jessica's discovery changed everything."

Professor Fergus reached out to take a sip from a coffee cup. "Jessica hit upon a formula to rectify genetic anomalies in nuclear cloning."

"What's that mean?" I asked.

"A formula to improve genetic imperfections." After I nodded to show I understood, he continued. "Jessica realized the enormous potential of her formula and agreed to Dr. Victor's proposal of testing it on human clones. But Jessica refused to divulge the exact nature of the formula, which angered Dr. Victor. Still, they went ahead with plans to work together in a secret laboratory."

"On the yacht," Varina said.

"Yes. Jessica felt energized by the ocean and arranged for the yacht with an unknown benefactor. Out of my respect for Jessica, I joined the project. I'd never seen her so excited before, and I was swept up in her high hopes. She wanted to find new ways to cure illnesses and ease human suffering, and she convinced me cloning would lead to great medical breakthroughs."

"Like super strength," I stated.

"Or my incredible eyesight," Eric said, pushing up the glasses he wore to stabilize his vision.

"But super skills aren't worth the downside of being a clone." Chase pursed his lips as if he was tempted to say more. Instead he glanced away with a dark look.

Professor Fergus took a deep breath, then went on, "I viewed human cloning as clinically as I did reproducing various strains of spinach. But Chase's miraculous creation changed me. He was going to be a short-term experiment, but when he squeezed my fingers and smiled at me, I realized I loved him like a son."

"Even knowing where my DNA came from?" Chase demanded.

"I didn't know the donor's actual identity, although I did know the type of person," he said carefully. "Dr. Victor acquired the necessary genetic materials."

"So for a trial run he created a disposable clone." Chase's jaw tightened, and his rugged features closed off all emotion.

"Jessica and I wouldn't let him hurt you."

"That was your mistake. You should have let Dr. Victor terminate me." His words chilled the room like a sudden arctic storm.

"So who is Chase cloned from?" I blurted out.

Professor Fergus frowned. "I'd rather not say."

"Still protecting me, Professor? Don't bother." Bitterness twisted like barbed wire in Chase's tone. "The truth is I was cloned from a serial killer. I don't know who he was, but sometimes I can feel his anger inside me ready to explode."

"You're not like that," Varina said softly.

All eyes were on Chase, and for long moments no one spoke. The tension built, and I squirmed in my chair.

I hated the silence, so I jumped in with the first thing that popped into my head. "Chase isn't the only one who knows about their clone donor." All eyes swiveled to me. "In fact, I spent today with her."

"You *what*?" Professor Fergus exclaimed. "You actually met that model? You can't be serious!"

"I—I am." I swallowed, startled by his harsh reaction. "I saw her picture in a magazine and wrote to her."

"I can't believe you'd do such a fool thing," he said angrily. "I warned you never to tell anyone you're a clone."

"But I didn't tell her, and she didn't act like she knew. She just thinks my resemblance is a coincidence."

"It's only a matter of time before she figures it out, and if the media or government finds out we'll all be in trouble." He blew out a deep breath, his expression weary. "Allison, you should have talked this over with me before writing that letter."

"I'm sorry. But you don't have to worry about Cressida. She's so much like me, and I know we can trust her even if she does find out. It was so great meeting her."

"She seemed pretty cool," Varina added with a supportive glance at me. "I can't see why it matters if Allison spends time with her."

"It's Dr. Victor we have to worry about," Chase stated.

"Yeah," I said, glad I hadn't mentioned being trapped in the dirt hole. Then the Professor would *really* have a reason to be mad at me. To ease his mind, I explained that Cressida was leaving town. "She's probably gone by now. And I doubt I'll see her again."

"Good," Eric said. "I didn't mind helping you find her, but I never really understood why you wanted to. It doesn't matter where our genes came from."

"Ah, but it *does* matter," Professor Fergus said, touching his fingers together as he regarded us seriously. "You kids weren't simply duplicated. You were improved. For example, Eric's donor was going blind, so the Enhance-X25 formula improved Eric's vision. There's a scientific term for improving human beings—"

"Eugenics." Eric sat up straighter in his chair and pushed up his glasses. "I read about it online when I was tracking down info on Dr. Victor. He wrote this creepy article on the benefits of creating perfect humans."

"But we aren't perfect," Varina pointed out. "I'm barely getting a B in my English class, and I'm hopeless at sports. When Starr and I play tennis, I always end up chasing the ball. I may have a great memory, but otherwise I'm just a regular kid."

"Yes. Thank goodness." Professor Fergus smiled fondly at his niece, then swept his gaze over the rest of us. "But all of you were born through artificial means; manipulated by science. And there's so much we have yet to learn." Professor Fergus leaned his elbows against his desk and gave us all searching looks. "From now on, I want you to take extra security precautions. Dr. Victor wants the Enhance-X25 formula, and he'll kill to get it. After his encounter with Varina, he probably suspects the formula worked—which means he's even more of a danger to us."

"But you don't have the formula," Chase said.

"I know that, but Dr. Victor doesn't believe it. So be on your guard at all times, and watch out for each other. Don't go anywhere alone."

His words chilled me, and I wondered if there was more to being a clone than I knew about. I knew that Eric still struggled to control his keen eyesight. Sometimes, he could see through walls or miles away, but other times, he grew dizzy and images blurred. And Varina wasn't sure if her memories were real or some kind of telepathic connection. Our powers were as mysterious as the threats that swirled around us.

Chase sat quietly in his chair, the hard edge returning to his expression as Professor Fergus continued talking about the experiments on the yacht.

The Professor's vivid words brought the past to life. Chase had been the first clone. His healthy progress caused the doctors to create four more clones with different personality types. The plan was to terminate the trial clone, then study the four new clones for several years until it became necessary to put them in a controlled foster-parent environment.

"Why did you give us numbers instead of names?" Varina interrupted, bending over to roll down her sock, revealing the tattoo: 1025G.

Eric pointed to his own ankle. "I'm 229B."

I didn't say anything since I had no tattoo, but I suspected I used to, because there was a scar on my ankle. My parents must have removed my tattoo through plastic surgery.

"I was against the tattooing, but Dr. Victor did it anyway. He used the donors' birth dates and added a B or a G to represent gender. Dr. Victor felt names caused emotional attachments." Remorse washed over the Professor's face. "But Jessica and I grew attached anyway.

Chase's tattoo was 611B, but we called him 'Six' and treated him like our own child. Every night, Jessica would sing him to sleep."

"I remember," Chase said simply.

"Jessica was a memorable lady." Professor Fergus smiled wistfully, and it dawned on me that he had loved her deeply.

"So what happened to Dr. Hart after she helped you rescue us?" I asked. "If she isn't dead, where is she?"

"That's the sixty-four-thousand-dollar question." Professor Fergus's gaze drifted to a large globe on a pedestal, and he frowned. "After Chase helped me settle the babies into the van I'd arranged, I drove Jessica to a hospital." His voice broke. "I—I had to leave her there. I couldn't stay, not with a five-year-old and four babies to care for."

"Us," Eric stated.

"Yes. You were all frightened and vulnerable, and I wanted to give you a chance at normal lives. So I spent a week anonymously leaving you at different adoption agencies: Allison in San Francisco, Chase in Nevada, Eric in Texas, and Sandee in Colorado. But when it came to leaving Varina, I just couldn't."

"I think I know why." Varina reached out and squeezed her uncle's hand. "It's because of my DNA donor."

"Yes." Professor Fergus nodded, his lips curving up in a ghost of a smile. "I loved all you children, but Varina was different. She was the last clone created, and since Dr. Victor was busy with other experiments, I chose her DNA donor. We'd already cloned a fashion model—"

"Cressida Ray," I put in.

Professor Fergus nodded. "We'd also cloned a computer expert and an Olympic athlete."

"Computer whiz over here." Eric flashed a goofy grin and waved his hand. "No way am I the Olympic type.

Not unless they have klutz competitions. Then I'm gold medal material."

I kicked Eric in the leg. Leave it to him to make jokes at such a serious moment.

"Yes, Eric," Professor Fergus said. "I do believe you share DNA with a computer expert and Sandee with the athlete, although as I mentioned before, I never knew the actual donors. Except one." He looked directly at his niece.

"Mine," Varina said with a tremble in her lips, as if she wasn't sure she wanted to hear more.

"Yes, honey. I gave into my sentimentality and chose a very special donor for you."

"I——I think I know who." Her voice was a whisper. "In my dreams, I talk to a woman with long red hair and green eyes like mine. I have a weird mental connection with her, and there's a good reason for it. Isn't there?"

He nodded, his face grim.

Chase, Eric, and I sat still, staring at Professor Fergus and Varina; anxious, curious, waiting.

"I was afraid to ask, but now I don't have to. I know who." Varina's words tumbled out. "I'm cloned from Dr. Jessica Hart."

FOURTEEN

Impossible. No way could I concentrate on the mundane act of doing my homework that night.

Images from the past and present distracted me. It was still weird to think that Varina, Eric, Chase, the missing Sandee, and I had spent our infancies in a secret laboratory on a yacht. I couldn't remember any of this, and yet I'd always felt a strong pull to the ocean; as if the crashing waves and screeching gulls tugged at my soul.

I'd finally told the Professor about my suspicious accident at the construction site. I quickly assured him it was probably just a freak thing, but he turned pale and frowned. He looked as if he was getting another of his bad headaches. I didn't dare mention what happened at the Rock Climbing Castle.

I didn't even tell Varina, Eric, or Chase, and usually I told them everything. But it was safer to keep this to myself for now. If someone was really trying to hurt me, I'd be careful. My strength had helped me escape before and it would protect me again if necessary.

At least, I hoped it would.

Besides, if Professor Fergus found out I'd been in danger, he'd forbid me to leave the house except for school. No more volunteer work. No more hanging out with my friends.

No thanks!

So after a long steaming bath, here I was tackling my homework. My algebra paper seemed to stare up at me, insisting I pay attention. But as I sat cross-legged on my bed, instead of calculating what Y times X equaled, I contemplated far more interesting equations.

Did Chase's DNA condemn him to a violent future? I guess it was the age-old "nature versus nurture" question. I'd always felt nature had more to do with personality, but now I wasn't so sure. Chase was *not* a killing machine. Sure he was a serious guy, but who wouldn't be after losing his parents? Besides, I'd seen his good side; his compassion, loyalty, and sense of humor. I refused to believe he was dangerous.

Mostly I felt sorry for him. Finding out he shared DNA with a killer had to be a major bummer. Poor Chase. I'd had a luckier toss of the DNA dice, was cloned from a model, not Charles Manson. Cressida was a wonderful "parent" donor. I already missed her.

Eric and Varina had done "DNA okay," too. Especially Varina. Dr. Hart sounded like a wonderful lady. No wonder Professor Fergus raised Varina as his own niece. He clearly had a major thing for Dr. Hart. Too bad they'd never gotten together. I bet they would have been a great couple.

Only, Dr. Hart disappeared from the hospital.

Poof! Totally gone.

Professor Fergus told us that a few weeks later, he'd received a cryptic letter from her. The postal stamp was from Santa Rosa, there was no return address, and the short note offered little information:

Dear J,
Cousin Tansy and I are fine. Don't worry.

Take care of our loved ones.

Always yours, J

Professor Fergus vaguely remembered Jessica's mentioning her cousin Tansy. But he didn't know where she lived or even her full name. He only knew Cousin Tansy lived alone and had a business called Sailor's Delight.

Unfortunately, in over a decade, there'd never been another communication from Dr. Hart.

With a long sigh, I forced my thoughts back to homework, and somehow managed to solve the mysteries of algebra Y's and X's. Then exhaustion won over excitement and I sunk into bed. I slept so deeply, I didn't awaken till my alarm went off.

After my incredible weekend, the ordinary rituals of Monday morning seemed out of sync. Yet I went through the motions: twisting my hair into a braid, sorting through my closet until I decided on my favorite denim overalls with a yellow shirt, then going downstairs to the kitchen and popping two halves of a cinnamon bagel in the toaster.

Typically, I was running late. Seymore High was only a few blocks away, but no matter how I strived for promptness, I continued to be late. Time-challenged, I called it.

Varina and Eric were always ahead of schedule, which irked me when I first moved here. In fact, early-bird Eric rose with the sun and took his dog Renegade for a walk every morning. His sense of humor showed one morning when he'd invited me to go along with him. At 5:30 A.M.! Like that would ever happen in this century—or even the next one!

"Your cinnamon toast smells good," someone said from behind me.

Glancing up, I saw Chase enter the kitchen. He flashed a warm smile, but that didn't mask his weary expression. I wondered if he'd had trouble sleeping.

"It's a bagel, not toast." I opened the fridge and took out strawberry cream cheese.

"So where's everyone?" he asked as he grabbed a bowl and spoon, a carton of milk, and a box of cereal before sitting at the kitchen table.

"Professor Fergus left twenty minutes ago for the college. And Eric and Varina are probably at school by now." Then I couldn't resist adding, "Varina hated leaving before you got up."

"Yeah. She's a good kid."

Only a "good kid"? I almost blurted out. Where was the romance in that statement? Nowhere. That was the problem. I wanted to tell Chase to get a clue, but loyalty to Varina kicked in and I zippered my lips. If she wasn't gonna tell Chase how she really felt about him, that was her choice.

My bagel popped up. After smearing it with cream cheese, I sat across from Chase at the table. "That was some intense meeting last night."

"Too intense." He frowned. "Afterward I felt like a jerk. I was out of line, blaming Uncle Jim for my flawed DNA."

"You're not flawed." I offered him an encouraging smile. "You're a great guy. And I know Varina would agree with me."

"You don't have any idea what I'm really like." He shook his head and poured cereal into a plastic bowl. "*I'm* not even sure."

"You're one of us and we all care about you." Especially Varina, I thought. Aloud I simply added, "That's all that matters."

"I care about you guys, too. That's the problem." He scowled. "I'm just extra baggage around here. I even blew it with Sandee Yoon. She's gone without a trace."

"She's the one who blew it. You tracked her down to Los Angeles, but she bailed before we could even meet her."

"Yeah. Although I never could figure out why."

"I read that note she left, and it's clear enough to me."

He blinked as he spooned a bite of cereal. "It is?"

I couldn't help but grin. Guys could be *so* dense. "You rescued Sandee from some serious bad guys. You were her hero. And she probably started thinking the two of you belonged together. Then she saw you with Varina. Jealousy alert!"

"Jealous? Of me and Varina?" He scrunched his forehead, still looking puzzled. "That's crazy."

"Are you sure?" I asked softly.

"Varina is special," he admitted. "When we talk, she really listens and understands. And when I was away, I missed her, wished she were there so we could talk. Maybe there's something between us, but I'm not sure of anything." His confusion mingled with sadness. "I only know I owe Professor Fergus a lot, and I'm gonna do my best to help find Dr. Hart."

"You have any ideas where to begin?"

"Not yet. But that letter is a good start. There can't be too many businesses called Sailor's Delight with an owner named Tansy. I'll make some calls while you're in school. It's not like I have anything better to do." He glanced away, his gaze sweeping outside. "Although I have been thinking about the future and making plans."

"What kind of plans?"

"Well, I'd like to go back to college. I had just started when . . ." He paused and glanced away. "Anyway, I can't just bum around forever. I want to work with nature or animals, maybe as a forest ranger. It's safer for me to be around wilderness, not people."

"College sounds like a good idea. California State University Sacramento isn't far away. Maybe you could apply there."

"No," he said sharply.

"Why not? If it's too expensive, I can help out."

"My parents left me enough money. That's not a

problem. I am." His gray-blue eyes glinted like steel. "I can't risk the violence inside me hurting anyone. That's why I've reached a decision."

"W-what?"

"As soon as Dr. Hart is found, I'm out of here. And I don't plan on ever coming back."

FIFTEEN

Chase's statement numbed me, and I didn't know what to say. Begging him to stay would never work. He was way too stubborn. Maybe Varina would have some ideas, since she knew him best.

We weren't supposed to go anywhere alone, so Chase dropped me off at Seymore High. As I waved good-bye to him, I heard the last bell ring.

Late again. Now I wouldn't be able to see Varina until after school, because we didn't share any classes or even the same lunch period. She's a sophomore and I'm a freshman, despite the fact that I'm a little older than her. But that's classified, top-secret clone information. Legally Varina is sixteen and I'm only fifteen. Professor Fergus altered her birth information when Varina was young to further disguise her from Dr. Victor's search. Great for her. Not so great for me.

I hurried to my homeroom class, adding another tardy slip to my growing collection.

Then I began the daily student three-step program:

#1: Sit. Listen. Paperwork.

#2: Go on to the next class.

#3: Repeat steps #1 and #2.

Multiply this process by six classes, and there went my day. It was hard to concentrate on lessons when my head was racing with plans for tracking down Dr. Hart, daydreams about Cressida, and worries for Chase.

When the final bell rang, announcing the end of school, I wanted to shoot fireworks into the sky. I skipped going to my own locker and went directly to the one Varina shared with Starr.

I found Varina there, as well as Starr and Eric.

Eric? But he usually walked home with his computer club buddies. I knew Starr was interested in him, but I hadn't expected her charms to work so quickly. It was weird to watch Eric's dopey expression as he gazed at Starr.

"You heard the great news?" Starr asked.

"Not yet," I said, shaking my head. "But I suspect I'm going to."

"That's for sure, girlfriend. Eric just asked me to the Sadie Hawkins Dance."

"Actually, *you* asked *me*," he pointed out with a grin. "And I said yes."

"That's 'cause you're smart enough to know a good thing when you see it," Starr said matter-of-factly. With anyone else this would have been bragging, but not Starr. That's just who she was.

"The dance sounds fun. Only it's not my thing so I won't be there," I admitted, not adding the real reason. Being almost six feet tall made it hard to find dance partners. Height was great if you were into basketball or modeling, but try dancing when your head towers above the crowd like Jack's beanstalk.

"Oh, are you gonna miss out! Hope you change your mind, Allison, and join us." Starr slammed her locker shut and then turned to Varina with a mischievous grin.

"Since Varina is my best friend, she *has* to go to the dance. We'll all go together."

"I'm not comfortable asking guys out," Varina said quickly.

"You only have to ask *one* guy. And if you're too chicken, I'll do it for you."

"No! I can do it myself!" Varina protested, her cheeks reddening. "There *is* a special guy I'd like to go with."

"Who?" Eric asked as he helped Starr fasten her backpack.

Varina hesitated a moment before finally admitting, "Chase. But he'd never go with me."

"How can you be sure unless you ask him?" Starr pointed out.

"He'd only say no. Although a dance might help him forget his problems and have fun for once."

Starr flashed her a knowing grin. "And you'd love to go out with him."

"More than anything. So I should at least try." Varina gave a wistful sigh as she picked up her backpack and slung it over her shoulders. "Okay. I'll do it. And if he says yes, I'll be the happiest girl in the universe."

Or the *un*happiest, I thought, when she found out Chase planned to leave town. The dance was almost two weeks away, and he'd probably be gone by then.

I wanted to warn Varina, but I didn't have the guts to crush her hopes. Not yet, anyway.

So I said I wanted to get an early start on homework, and hurried away from my friends.

When I reached the house, I noticed the empty driveway. Good—Professor Fergus wouldn't complain about my walking home from school alone. He was probably still at the college, maybe giving a makeup test or attending a staff meeting.

Chase's Ford truck was missing, too. My heart tightened, and for a moment I wondered if he'd already left.

Then I remembered he was searching for information on Dr. Hart. He'd probably show up later.

I walked to the front door and found it locked. So I dug out my key from my pocket, twisted the knob, and went inside.

There was an eerie hush throughout the house, my own footsteps making a soft *clomp-clomp* sound on the foyer tile. I slipped off my backpack and it thudded to the floor. I paused, having a creepy "all alone" feeling.

I knew that Varina and Eric would be joining me soon, filling the house with ordinary noises. But I didn't like being alone, and I thought of Eric's dog, Renegade. The yellow Lab was always eager for attention.

Leaving my backpack on the floor, I entered the kitchen and headed for the side door that led into the backyard.

The phone rang, its shrill bell reverberating through the house. Automatically, I reached for the kitchen wall phone.

"Fergus residence," I greeted.

"May I speak with the Professor?" a man with a low rolling Hispanic accent asked.

"I'm sorry, but he's not here. Would you like to leave a message?"

There was a pause, then a gruff question: "Whom am I speaking to?"

"Allison. And you are . . . ?" I waited for his reply, reaching across the kitchen counter to grab a message pad and a pen. "Okay, I have pen and paper. Who's calling?"

"Dr. Mansfield Victor."

I gasped. My legs nearly buckled, and I sagged against the counter.

"So you've heard of me?" he asked with an eerie chuckle. "You must be the blond subject. 330G."

Chills tingled my skin and my stomach churned. "I don't know what you mean."

"Don't you?" Another chuckle. "For some time now, I've kept track of you and your friends."

My grip on the phone grew so tight, I was afraid I might crush it. But I had to keep my cool and pretend I didn't know what he was talking about. "You must have the wrong number."

"Don't waste time on games. Tell Professor Fergus I'm willing to double my offer. But I won't be patient much longer."

"Leave him alone!"

"I will. When I get what I want." He paused, then added darkly, "I'm sure you know what I'm referring to."

"I don't know anything. Just that you're some creep bagging on the Professor." My hand on the phone trembled with rage. "Stop harassing Professor Fergus or I'll—"

"Tough words for a little girl. What could you possibly do?" he taunted, clearly enjoying this cat-and-mouse game.

"I could do a lot," I said evasively. "And the Professor doesn't have what you want, so just leave us alone."

Then I slammed down the phone.

Shaking, I leaned against the kitchen counter and waited for my heart to slow. I'd talked tough, but inside I was totally Jell-O.

I stepped across the room to the table, pulled out a chair, and wearily sank down on the polished wood. Now I understood why Professor Fergus had been so upset. Dr. Victor reeked of evil. In the name of science, he would kill whoever stood in his way.

My gaze drifted around the room, taking in the ordinary things that connected me to normalcy: the chrome toaster, the double-door refrigerator, the microwave, and the sink that still had breakfast dishes in it.

Dr. Victor's threats didn't change anything around me, and yet I felt changed. My enemy now had a voice.

He wasn't just a vague menace I'd been warned about.

He was real.

As soon as Professor Fergus came home, I'd tell him about the call. Part of me wanted to keep quiet, but the other part knew that Dr. Victor wouldn't give up. He would call back, so I had to warn the Professor.

A sudden shrill sound blared.

I gasped and gripped the back of my chair. I froze with new fear. The phone was ringing . . . again.

SIXTEEN

The phone rang for a second and third time.

I couldn't move. Frankly, I didn't want to. I wasn't ready for another nasty encounter with Dr. Victor.

A fourth ring blared.

I swallowed hard. Then I forced myself to cross the room. Before the phone could ring a fifth time, I grabbed the receiver and exclaimed, "I told you not to call here ever again!"

"Excuse me?" the caller said in a gentle voice that was definitely not Dr. Victor's.

"Cressida!" I exclaimed, a rush of embarrassment mingling with joy. "I—I'm so sorry. . . . I thought it was someone else."

"I'm glad I'm not *that* person." She laughed, the sound light and musical to my ears. "But I know how irritating those persistent sales calls can be."

"Yeah. They can be really annoying."

"So you should screen them with caller ID. Or use a phone machine or voice mail. I'm fortunate Dolores takes my calls. She's overbearing, but an efficient manager."

"Sorry for greeting you so rudely. Such a lame mistake."

"No problem. I understand."

"Are you in Chicago?"

"No. We canceled the trip. Plans have changed." There was a rush of excitement in her tone. "That's what I'm calling you about."

I stretched the coiled phone cord across the kitchen counter and sat in a chair. "So where are you?"

"At the Winter Crest Inn."

"No way! But that's here in town. Cool!" I didn't bother hiding my delight. Maybe I *would* see Cressida again. Things were looking up.

"I was supposed to be in Chicago. I mean, all the arrangements were made and my suitcases were packed," the model went on. "But then my agent had this incredible idea."

"What?"

"After meeting you, Jackson couldn't talk about anything else. He was totally blown away with your resemblance to me and he actually wanted to know if you were my secret daughter."

"He did?" I choked out.

"Of course I told him that was impossible." She chuckled. "I've only been married once, and it was to him. He certainly would have known if I ever had a child. Besides, I'm too young to have a teenage daughter."

I knew from magazine articles that she was almost forty, which was plenty old to have a daughter my age. But I didn't point this out. Having a career where youth and beauty were celebrated probably made her insecure about getting older.

"Anyway, Jackson kept talking about you. How you sounded, moved, and looked like me," she continued in the same light and fluffy whipped-cream tone. "And he came up with the most incredible idea."

I was half-afraid to ask, but I did anyway. "What?"

"You know I'm the spokeswoman for Comfort skin cream?"

"Yeah."

"Well, the Comfort people want a new look for their next ad campaign. So Jackson got on the phone and pitched them a past-and-future scenario. A young girl using Comfort on her skin, then jump forward about ten years. Now the girl is a woman with the same youthful skin."

"Sounds cool."

"I knew you'd think so. It'll be an incredible shoot. I'll be the youthful woman and you'll be the young girl. Don't you just love the idea?"

"Wait a minute. *Me? A model?*"

"Sure. Why not?"

"Uh, I don't have any experience." I tried to think of a tactful way to say I'd rather haul garbage than model.

"I'll teach you everything. Think of all the fun we'll have, Allison."

"I don't know."

"It'll be a blast! We'll spend a lot of time together and get to know each other well. We'll go shopping, dine at the best restaurants, and maybe even try something adventurous—"

"Not rock climbing again!"

"Been there, done that. But bungee jumping sounds exciting." Then she laughed and I knew she was teasing me. Even our sense of humor was alike. "Okay, forget the adventure. But hey, we can find some time for a movie."

"Yeah." I gave a wistful sigh. "I'd like that."

"If we wore the same outfits and fixed our hair alike, people would think we're twins, or sisters. I've always wanted a sister."

"Me too." My heart tugged with longing, and the phrase "Modeling sucks the big one" stuck in my throat.

I wasn't wild about modeling, but if she enjoyed it so much it couldn't be too bad.

Then again, my opinion of modeling didn't really matter. There were other reasons I couldn't agree with the plan.

"I'm sorry, Cressida," I said sincerely. "But it's not going to work."

"Why not?"

"I have other things to do. Like go to school."

"But you won't miss more than a day or two. I'll speak to your principal and explain the situation."

"No." I shook my head firmly. "There's a test coming up in algebra. I'm not sure when it's scheduled, and my grades aren't good enough to miss it."

"I hated math when I was your age. But no worry. Dolores is a numbers whiz and she can help you study. If you miss the test, I'll arrange for you to take a makeup test."

"I—I'm not sure—"

"You probably won't even miss the test," she cut in. "The photographer can't fly in till Wednesday, so we won't start work until Thursday." She paused and added, "Please, Allison. It would mean so much to me."

I didn't know what to say. I wanted to spend time with her. Although I was the dirt-under-my-fingernails type, her dazzling glamour intrigued me. We were identical and yet so different. I think the differences intrigued me more than the similarities. She'd experienced so much more of the world than I had. Maybe by getting to know Cressida, I could learn more about myself—the person I'd become someday.

So instead of replying with a firm no, I wavered and copped out, saying I'd ask Professor Fergus. This delighted Cressida, but made me feel guilty. I knew the Professor wouldn't approve. He'd made it clear how he felt about my friendship with Cressida.

Too risky.

As I hung up the phone, I heard the front door open and Eric and Varina's voices.

"Hey, Allison, where's Chase?" was Varina's first question as she entered the kitchen.

"I don't know." I shrugged, sitting still and a bit numb at the table. I couldn't get Cressida's words out of my head. "Please give modeling a chance. This means so much to me."

And *she* meant a lot to me.

But modeling? Posing like a Barbie doll in a glossy dollhouse setting? It just wasn't going to happen.

"I bet Chase is looking for Dr. Hart and Cousin Tansy," Eric told Varina as he opened the fridge and grabbed a can of root beer and an apple. "That's what we should get cracking on, too."

"You're right," I agreed.

"I'll do whatever I can to find Jessica. I'm so worried about her." Varina sank in a chair beside me and frowned. "I haven't dreamed about her since she warned of danger."

"Too bad your dreams can't tell us where she is," I said.

"They're always so vague, just her voice and a foggy image of her face. Once I thought I smelled the ocean and another time I smelled smoke, but I might have imagined it."

"Finding someone who vanished so long ago is practically impossible," I complained. "Where do we start? We don't even know Tansy's last name."

There was the thud of heavy footsteps, and then a new voice rang out, "Oh, yes we do."

I looked up as Chase strode into the room. I hadn't even heard him come into the house, but you can bet with those sharp ears of his, he'd heard us. He could hear conversations as far away as Seymore High if he concentrated hard enough.

His white-blond hair was windblown and his gray-blue eyes shone with excitement. "I've been at libraries and government buildings all day, and I managed to track down the Sailor's Delight."

"Great!" Eric pulled up a chair and sat beside me, setting his root beer on the table.

"It took a while, but finally I found Tansy's full name."

"So what is it?" I asked.

Chase pulled a crumpled paper from his pocket and read off, "Tansy Irene Norris. I was hoping for a more unusual last name, something easy to track down, but knowing her full name will be a great help."

"Now all we need is her address," Eric said. "Or did you find that, too?"

"I found the Sailor's Delight address, but not hers."

"The business address should be good enough," Varina said, pushing back her auburn hair. "When we find Tansy, hopefully we'll find Jessica Hart, too."

"Let's go upstairs and check my computer." Eric rose and headed for the doorway. "I'll search the web for both Tansy Irene Norris and the Sailor's Delight."

"Sounds good," Chase approved.

"I hope his cyber hocus-pocus leads us to Dr. Hart soon—before Dr. Victor finds her," Varina said.

"If he already hasn't." I paused and then added grimly, "He called here a while ago."

"He did?" Chase practically growled.

"Yeah. He wanted the Professor. He really creeped me out—calling me 'the blond one' and mentioning a number like the ones you guys have tattooed on your ankle. 330G, I think." I paused, trying to remember what the Professor had told us about the tattooed codes. They represented our DNA donor's birthday. Did that mean Cressida's birthday was March 30?

"Dr. Victor scares me," Varina admitted.

"If he tries to hurt you again, he'll be sorry." Chase

balled his fist and smacked it in his other hand. "That scumbag deserves to suffer."

I cringed at the violence in Chase's voice. "Dr. Victor seems more interested in finding the formula than in going after us. And when he realizes the Professor doesn't have the formula, he'll go after Dr. Hart."

"Then we'll have to find her before he does," Eric said.

A short while later, we were gathered in his upstairs bedroom around his computer. Eric worked deftly, his fingers flying across the keyboard. Varina, Chase, and I sat on the edge of Eric's bed, quiet and waiting. While Varina and Chase sat close and spoke to each other in low intimate tones, my gaze wandered around the room. Dangling stars and planet mobiles swirled from the ceiling, and a rainbow-hued clown costume hung on a wall hook. Eric was a mix of serious and slapstick, occasionally twisting colorful balloons while wearing a clown outfit to entertain sick or disadvantaged kids.

"I found something," Eric suddenly announced.

Immediately, Chase, Varina, and I jumped up and crossed the room to peer over Eric's shoulder. The computer screen glowed with a long list of names, addresses, and other data.

"That looks like an official government file. How'd you get it?" Chase asked, pointing at the screen.

"Don't ask." Eric twisted his head to face us with a wry smile. "I don't approve of hacking, but sometimes it's the only choice. And this is for a good cause."

Scanning down the screen, I stopped when I saw the name "Tansy I. Norris." There was a whole list of financial and personal information. "That's her!" I exclaimed.

"Good work, Eric," Varina added, patting his shoulder.

"It's easy enough. Too easy, really. No one has any

privacy these days." Eric hit a few keys and the printer gave a shrill beep, then began printing out. "Her personal phone number isn't listed, but her business number is. The Sailor's Delight is near Bodega Bay. That's about a two-hour drive from here."

"It's too late to go tonight," Chase said practically. "But I can check it out tomorrow while you guys are in school."

"No fair leaving us behind!" Varina complained.

"But you don't get out of school till three o'clock. I can go there and be back by then."

"Not without us." Eric gave Chase a deep look. "We're in this together."

"Yeah," I said. "If we leave directly from school, we can reach Bodega Bay by five. That's not too late."

Chase gave an exasperated shake of his blond head. Then he shrugged. "Okay. I'll pick you up after school tomorrow." He pointed his finger at me. "And I'm not waiting around, so don't be late."

"Me, late? Never happen." I laughed, reminding myself to never show Chase my collection of tardy slips. "I'll be there at three tomorrow. And that's a promise."

SEVENTEEN

When Professor Fergus returned home, he was impressed we'd found Cousin Tansy's address when his previous attempts had yielded nothing. Hope reflected in his tired eyes. And I noticed that when he walked down the hall into his office, he wasn't leaning as heavily on the cane.

It was great to see him feeling better, but now I was even more reluctant to tell him about the call from Dr. Victor. Still, he needed to be forewarned, so after washing the dinner dishes while Eric dried and put them away, I faced the Professor in his office.

"Sorry to bother you," I began timidly, twisting the end of my blond braid.

"I'm not very busy right now." He set his reading glasses on his desk next to a pile of papers and gave me a warm smile. "What's on your mind?"

"Someone called for you today."

"Who?" he asked curiously, his graying brows knitting together.

"Dr. Victor." I recounted the conversation to the best

of my memory, then tensed, watching his reaction. His skin blanched and his jaw tensed. He seemed especially bothered that Dr. Victor knew who I was.

"At least he didn't mention my strength," I added.

"Which is good. But if he's been spying on me, he may suspect you kids have unusual abilities." Professor Fergus leaned forward at his desk and idly tapped the wood with a pencil. "As infants, none of you showed any signs of amazing powers. This infuriated Dr. Victor, because he expected quick results from the Enhance-X25 formula. He wanted to do more drastic experiments—painful tests unfit for small children. Naturally, Jessica and I stopped him."

"Thank goodness!" I exclaimed with a shudder. The Professor had really been there for us. But I hadn't been entirely truthful with him. So I sucked in a deep breath, blew it out, and confessed, "There was also another phone call."

"Oh?" He arched an eyebrow.

"From Cressida Ray."

"The model? What did she want?"

"Me." I gave a half-smile, then went on to explain about the proposed modeling shoot.

"Of course you told her no."

His tone irked me, and resentment flared. "I told her I wasn't sure."

"Well, you can't do it."

"Why not? I promised not to tell anyone about being a clone, and I meant it."

"But with Dr. Victor threatening us, you need to be extra careful."

"There will be tons of people around a modeling shoot. I'll be perfectly safe."

"I didn't realize you were interested in modeling." He stroked his salt-and-pepper beard as he gazed at me.

"Not exactly. But I want to know Cressida. It may be my only chance to be with the one person in the whole world who really understands me. She even offered to arrange to get my school assignments and tutoring."

"I'm here if you need tutoring."

"I know, and I appreciate it."

"But this isn't about schoolwork," he added with a sigh. "This is really important to you, isn't it?"

"Cressida is. It's like finding my long-lost twin, but then being forced apart. If I don't spend time with her and I never see her again, I'll regret it for the rest of my life. We're alike in so many ways. She even told me she loves the same kind of sandwiches I do—pickle and peanut butter."

"It's only logical you'd share many traits. But you have to realize she's a grown woman with a completely different lifestyle. You don't know her well enough to trust her."

"Yes I do." I paused and lifted my chin. "I'd trust her with my life."

"Let's hope it doesn't come to that," he said grimly. He paused and gave me a deep look. "I suppose if you want to spend some time with her, I won't stand in your way."

"Great!" I jumped up joyfully.

"But on one condition: I don't mind if you're with her, but I have to put my foot down on modeling. It's out of the question."

"Well . . ." I sighed. "I'm not the modeling type anyway."

"And it's too dangerous. We don't need the public seeing pictures of you next to your clone." He reached for some papers and donned his reading glasses again, ending our talk.

As I left the room, I moved slowly, torn between disappointment and relief. I dreaded telling Cressida I couldn't model with her. I hoped she'd understand.

But most of all, I hoped that my getting to know her was the right decision, and not the biggest mistake of my entire life.

EIGHTEEN

The next day at school moved even slower than the day before. I kept thinking about Cressida. When I'd called to tell her that my answer on my doing the shoot was no, she'd seemed disappointed. She sighed, then admitted that Jackson had come up with a different idea for the Comfort shoot anyway.

Then she brightened and came up with an alternate plan. I wouldn't model, but I could be her assistant. Also, she wanted some keepsake photos of me, so, she pointed out as if to console me, I'd be spending some time in front of a camera after all. But the photos were for her private album, so I didn't bother mentioning it to the Professor.

When Cressida talked excitedly about how much fun we'd have, I actually forgot who I was for a moment, and felt as if I were her sister, close friend, or daughter. I wondered what it would be like to really be like her. A model.

Imagining myself on a runway in high heels and slinky clothes made me smile. I wasn't sure whether to laugh or shake my head at this fantasy. But the tiny seeds were planted in my mind and I found myself moving through the school halls in a gliding stride rather than my usual leisurely clomp. When I'd see my reflection in a window, I'd straighten up and toss my braid back over my shoulder, imagining bright lights and camera flashes catching my every move.

And still the day crept by on snail slime.

Finally, the last bell of the day rang.

I raced for my locker, planning to just make a quick stop; no way would I keep Chase waiting. In fact, I planned to be there before Eric and Varina.

But when I spun my lock combination and opened my locker, I saw something odd: a long yellow envelope poking like a flag between my history and English books.

"What's this?" I murmured as I reached for the envelope.

My name was typed neatly on the front.

A prickly sensation hit me, and I quickly turned around to see if someone was watching. Did I have a secret admirer? Or maybe Eric was playing a practical joke and when I opened the envelope Silly String would spring out.

But I didn't see Eric, only strangers and casual friends who swarmed up and down the halls, paying no attention to me. So with my lips pressed together in concentration, I ripped open the envelope.

A single square of paper fluttered out. I bent down to retrieve it, then read the short poisonous message.

Dead clones don't tell secrets.

NINETEEN

Dead clones!

Dr. Victor's phone call had been scary, but this threatening note was far worse. That creepy doctor was totally psycho, and I trembled, knowing deep in my soul that he wouldn't rest until he had what he wanted.

My heart was pounding loud enough to jump off the Richter scale, and I wanted to cry out for help. But I pressed my lips tightly together so no sound could escape. I'd never been the crying type, and I wasn't about to start now just because of some sicko note. I could handle this on my own, just as I'd handled every other crisis in my life. I wouldn't let Dr. Victor reduce me to a quivering mass of fear.

Assuming the note *had* come from Dr. Victor. But if not him, then who?

Why would someone threaten me at school? And how had they snuck the note into my locker? Either they'd broken into it somehow or had been lurking close enough to spy on me as I spun my combination. Was I being watched right now? And if the culprit was Dr.

Victor, why would he warn me *not* to tell secrets? He wanted to know my secrets, not prevent me from revealing them. The message didn't make any sense.

I stood on shaky legs, unsure what to do. Who should I turn to? My clone friends? Professor Fergus? The police? But if I told the police, I'd have to explain about being a clone.

"Allison!" I heard someone call my name. Turning around, I saw Dustin waving at me as he hurried forward.

"Oh, no!" I cried, slipping the threatening note back in the envelope and shoving it in an overall pocket. He'd been dogging me all day, pestering me about Professor Fergus's "school" and asking pointed questions about why he couldn't sign up for tutoring. He could cause big trouble for us if he kept digging for information. Major problem.

But I was too freaked out over the threatening note to deal with Dustin, too. So the best course was avoidance. I zigzagged down a few halls, then paused to catch my breath, looking around for an escape route. The girls' rest room was down at the end of the hallway, so I raced toward it.

I coughed at the whiff of smoke that lingered in the small room. One door was shut, and underneath it I glimpsed white sandals and blue-painted toenails.

Turning on the faucet, I pretended to wash my hands. I wondered if Dustin was outside waiting for me. Probably. How long would he wait before giving up?

Glancing at my watch, I groaned. I was already late! Oh, no! And I'd promised Chase I'd be on time.

The stall door opened and a chubby girl with a nose ring walked over to the sinks. I didn't know her, but she seemed okay.

"Would you check outside and see if a thin brown-haired guy is still there?" I asked her.

"Sure." She grinned. "You ditching your boyfriend?"

"He's not my boyfriend, just a pest." I grimaced. "I wish he'd just give up and leave me alone."

"I can sympathize. Guys are always after me, too." She patted my shoulder as she crossed to the door. She peeked outside and gave me a thumbs-up signal. "All clear."

I thanked her, then hurried outside. Dustin was gone. But I was later than ever. As I ran through the halls, out of the school, toward the parking lot, I crossed my fingers and hoped Chase had waited.

But when I reached the parking lot, I didn't see his truck. I pushed back my windblown bangs and bit my lip. I was too late. Darn that Dusty Stiff-Bottom anyway!

My shoulders slumped, disappointment weighing them down more than my heavy backpack ever could. I was also uneasy, wondering if whoever had sent the threatening letter was nearby.

There wasn't much else I could do except head home.

Just as I reached the sidewalk, I heard several sharp honks. Turning around, hoping to see Chase's truck, I saw a gray sedan, and someone inside waving at me!

TWENTY

I blinked and stared in surprise. Chase sat behind the wheel of Professor Fergus's midsize sedan, with Varina beside him and Eric in the backseat.

"Thanks for waiting," I said with great relief as I slipped inside beside Eric. "But what happened to your truck?"

"Nothing," Chase replied with a grin.

Varina twisted around to face me. "Uncle Jim got home early and offered his car. Chase's truck was too small for the four of us. This is much more comfortable."

"Cool!" I was still shaking inside, but I managed to sound calm. "I wondered how we would all squeeze in Chase's truck."

"Professor Fergus came through for us again," Chase said.

"My uncle is the best." Varina grinned.

I nodded.

Eric gave me a probing look. "Allison, what's wrong?"

"Nothing, except I was afraid you'd leave without me."

"It's more than that. You're scared." Eric's dark eyes met mine in a "Don't feed me that bull" look. "What's up?"

Varina and Chase were now staring at me, too. I sighed. What was the use?

So I reached into my pocket and showed them the envelope.

"OH, NO!" Varina cried after reading it. "Someone knows."

"It has to be Dr. Victor." Chase's dark brows knit together ominously. "As long as he's alive, he'll never leave us alone. I'm going to find him and—"

"You'll do nothing," Varina ordered, putting a hand on Chase's shoulder.

Chase scowled, then turned around swiftly.

Fear, frustration, and tension filled the car, and I wished I'd never showed them the letter.

"Hey, chill, guys. This dumb note doesn't scare me." I gave a weak laugh. "If that's the worst Dr. Victor can do, he's pathetic."

"Allison's right," Eric put in. "We're the ones with powers. Dr. Demented wouldn't stand a chance against us."

"Don't underestimate him," Chase warned. He changed the subject by reaching for a map, then handing it to Varina. "We better get going. You can navigate."

"Fine." She unfolded the map. "We may hit some traffic, but otherwise it'll be an easy drive. I hope we find Tansy. Maybe we should have called first."

"No." Chase turned the wheel, increasing his speed slowly as he pulled out of the parking lot. "I'd rather take her by surprise. Then she can't avoid our questions."

"But what if we drive all the way and Tansy isn't

even there?" Varina persisted. "She could be on vacation, or a business trip."

"Then we'll have had a fun trip to the ocean," Eric said optimistically.

"We can hike around Goat Rock Beach," I added.

"Oh, I almost forgot," Chase suddenly said when the car stopped at a crosswalk. The angry edge to his voice was gone, which was a relief. He reached for a pile of papers on his dash. "Just as I left, the mail arrived. I know Eric is always eager for letters from his family, so I brought it along. But I haven't gone through it. Go for it, Eric."

"Thanks!" Eric took the bundle of letters and assorted junk mail. "Hey, here's a coupon for a free deodorant sample. You can have it, Allison." He tossed the slim paper into my lap.

I rolled my eyes. "Oh, thanks."

"And there are *two* letters from Texas," Eric declared. "One from my parents and the other from my sister Kristyn."

"Great. Kristyn must be doing better," I said hopefully. Kristyn had been kidnapped several months ago, and the experience had scarred her emotionally. Eric felt responsible, which was partly why he'd decided to move to California.

Eric was still sorting through the mail. Suddenly he came to a rectangular postcard and gave a low whistle. "Hey, here's one for Chase."

"Me? Must be a mistake." Chase glanced at us through the rearview mirror, his gray-blue eyes wide with surprise. "I haven't given anyone that address."

"You must have," Eric said with an odd expression. "Or else she wouldn't have known to write there."

"Who?" I asked, leaning over and peering at the postcard. When I saw the signature, my mouth fell open and I cried, "Ohmygosh! It's from Sandee Yoon!"

TWENTY-ONE

"Sandee!" Chase exclaimed, his grip on the steering wheel taut. "You're kidding."

"No joke. Want me to read it to you?" I asked, dying of curiosity but fighting the temptation to peek.

Chase's furrowed brows reflected in the rearview mirror. "Now that I think back, I did give her the Ferguses' old address."

I checked the postcard. "Well she must have figured out we moved, because she mailed it to the present address."

"Really?" Chase asked with a hint of admiration. "Still, I don't know why she's writing after all this time. But who could figure a girl like that out? She's not like anyone I ever met before."

I saw Varina roll her eyes.

"So can I read the postcard?" I persisted.

Chase shrugged. "Go ahead."

"Yes!" I grinned, glancing at the picture on the card of a chimpanzee swinging upside down from a tree, his mouth stretched open in a huge laugh. There was no caption, but if there had been, I bet it would have said, "I made a monkey out of you!"

Because that's exactly what Sandee did to Chase. She'd lied to him about her identity when they first met. He'd helped her get away from some bad dudes, and she'd repaid him by taking off, leaving only a note behind—a note that revealed her real identity. And until now there'd been no news of her.

As Chase left the suburban streets and merged onto the freeway, I cleared my throat and started to read aloud.

"Dear Chase," I began. "Surprise! Wanted to let you know I'm doing great. I mean: GREAT! I've got a new name and a cool singing gig. And no one's gonna find me, so don't bother trying. I don't need you or anyone else. Bye—Sandee."

"That's all?" Eric asked with disappointment.

"Yeah." I turned it over and looked at the laughing monkey. I knew that somewhere Sandee was laughing at us, too.

"Did she include an address?" Chase glanced to the backseat where I sat beside Eric, then quickly returned his attention to driving.

"No address. And the postmark is from Colorado."

"Colorado?" Eric's dark eyes widened. "She went back home?"

"Or she had a friend mail this for her," I guessed. "I doubt she'd return to her foster family."

"Can't blame her for that," Chase said.

I remembered the quick trip Chase and I had taken to Colorado when we'd been searching for Sandee. I'd met Sandee's foster mother: a sharp-tongued woman who smelled like alcohol and didn't hide her dislike for Sandee. At the time, I'd felt sorry for Sandee, understanding why she'd run away from such a dysfunctional home. But now I wasn't so sure.

"I'm glad Sandee is doing okay," I said with a sigh. "Only I wish she'd given us a chance."

"We don't need her," Varina said. "So what if she's a clone? She doesn't care about anyone but herself. She only sent this postcard to bug Chase."

"Or to let him know she was safe," Eric said.

"I doubt it." Varina glanced at Chase protectively, although he didn't seem to notice as he drove quietly, focusing on the road and not the conversation. "Chase worked hard finding her, helped her out of a bad situation, then she repaid him by ditching him."

"Yeah," I agreed. "A total ingrate."

"What's with you girls?" Eric demanded. "Is this Dump on Sandee Day?"

"She deserves it," Varina said.

"I can't believe you aren't more compassionate. Sandee's had it tough. Give her a break."

In which arm? I was tempted to say, but Eric's reproachful expression sobered me. Maybe I *was* being too hard on Sandee.

"At least we know about our pasts," Eric went on, his seat belt straining as he leaned forward. "But Sandee doesn't even know she's a clone."

"That's got to be hard." I thought for a moment, twisting my braid around my finger. "She's probably freaking out over some weird power. I wonder what. Maybe she can run fast. After all, she keeps running away, and no one can catch her," I couldn't resist saying.

From the front seat, Varina turned around and grinned at me. "That's for sure."

"Can we just talk about something else?" Chase suddenly snapped, roughly changing lanes and increasing his speed. "You never even met Sandee. You don't know anything about her."

"I know enough," Varina retorted.

"No you don't. None of you do. So just cut out the snide remarks."

"Well, *excuse us,*" Varina said in a sharp, hurt tone. "I didn't realize you cared so much for Sandee."

"I care that I failed to help her."

"You tried. She's the one who bailed."

"I should have explained things to her right away. She's gone, and it's my fault. So let's just drop it."

"My pleasure," Varina snapped.

I could only see the back of Varina's head, but by her stiff neck and sudden interest in watching scenery, I knew she was steaming. And I didn't blame her. She'd been gathering courage to ask Chase to the Sadie Hawkins Dance, and then he'd started acting all weird about Sandee. I wondered if more had gone on between Sandee and Chase than we knew about. Had they held hands, shared confidences, or maybe even kissed?

For Varina's sake, I hoped not.

Chase turned the radio on, but even the lively music couldn't ease the suffocating silence in the car. After a while, Eric filled the empty air by ripping open his letters and sharing chatty news from Texas. It was fun hearing about his large, busy family—so very different from my childhood. As Eric shared his news, I noticed the catch in his voice. Poor guy wouldn't admit it, but I could tell he was homesick.

My gaze drifted out the window to rolling hills March dressed in lush green and pastures filled with cows and occasional horses or llamas. As we neared the coast, the oak trees thinned out, replaced by towering rows of dark green eucalyptus trees. And a strong, moist, salty tang filled the air. There were fewer cars on the two-lane road, and only a scattering of homes.

"Just a few more miles," Chase announced. "What's the address we're looking for?"

"242 Gull Street," Eric said, referring to his computer printout. "I ran a cyber map search and have the directions." He pointed up ahead. "There's your turnoff. Make a left at the first street."

"Got it," Chase replied, smoothly turning the wheel.

In the distance, beyond hills and homes, I glimpsed a speck of blue water, and felt a strong urge to get close to the ocean. I hoped it didn't take long to find Tansy so there'd be time to go to the beach, too.

We turned onto Gull Street a few minutes later, and I started looking for an address.

"There's number 125," I said, pointing at a narrow white house with a peaked roof and an attached garage holding a gleaming blue boat.

"Not too much farther," Varina murmured.

"There's number 210," Eric said excitedly. "Tansy's place should be on the next block."

The buildings were closer together now, some of them homes and some businesses: Mandy's Market, Salty's Antiques, a beauty salon called Permanent Waves.

"Hey, that last place's address was 254 Gull Street," Chase said, turning his head back and forth as he stared out the window. "How did I miss it?"

"Let's go back and check again," Eric suggested. "It has to be there."

Chase made a U-turn and we slowly drove past the buildings. When we came to 240 Gull Street, a craft shop called Sea Escapes, Chase stopped the car.

Our gazes all turned toward the lot next door. At first I thought the lot was empty, until I noticed the charred ruins of a building. And then I saw a small metal sign lying by a pile of ashes. The sign was bent and the letters faded, but I could vaguely make out two words.

Sailor's Delight.

We'd found Tansy's business. Too late.

Without a word, we stepped out of the car and stood in a small group on the broken sidewalk. We just stared, as if this were a somber funeral. And maybe it was.

An acrid stench filled the air. I realized that this was a recent fire.

"Jessica warned of danger," Varina whispered as she

reached out and squeezed my hand. Her skin was clammy and chilled.

"I wonder what happened to Tansy," I said in a hushed tone. "I hope she wasn't here when the fire broke out. That she isn't . . ." There was no need to finish the sentence.

"Me too," Varina said, nodding. "But what about Jessica? What if Dr. Victor already found her?"

Chase came over and patted Varina gently on the shoulder. She didn't push away, so I guessed everything was okay between them again. "Dr. Hart will be fine," he assured us.

"I hope so."

"Me too."

There was a crunch of footsteps behind us, and suddenly someone yelled, "Get away from there!"

Whirling around, I saw a rough-looking, stocky woman with dark hair tucked under a cap and dressed in a loose plaid shirt over worn jeans and heavy army boots.

But it wasn't her appearance that caught my attention. It was the rifle she was pointing at us.

TWENTY-TWO

"You're trespassing," the woman accused.

"Sorry." I froze. "We didn't mean to."

"And I won't mean to shoot you. But if you don't get back in your car and skedaddle, my trigger finger might slip."

"We're here for a good reason," Eric said hastily. "We're looking for the woman who used to work here."

"No one here now except insects and ghosts. This is private property. So don't even think about poking through what's left of this sorry place."

"We would never!" Varina protested.

Chase stepped forward, offering a calm smile. He gestured to the charred rubble. "Can you tell us what happened here?"

"I could, if I had a mind to. Who are you, anyway?"

"I'm Chase Rinaldi." He pointed and added, "My friends are Allison Beaumont, Eric Prince, and Varina Fergus."

The woman's gaze lingered on Varina for a brief moment, then she swiveled back to Chase. "I'm Reena

Bond, owner of Sea Escapes." She pointed to the ocean-themed novelty shop next door.

"Then you must know the Sailor's Delight owner, Tansy Norris," I put in eagerly. "We really need to talk to her."

"Sailor's Delight is history now." Then she narrowed her eyes, as if assessing us, and gave a shake of her head. "It was a fine gift shop, too, before the fire. A real tragedy."

"I'm sorry," Eric said solemnly.

"It's not *my* loss. My business wasn't touched." She pointed to Sea Escapes. "Although I do feel bad about Tansy."

"What happened to her?" Varina asked in a fearful voice. "I hope she's all right."

"That's for angels to tell," the woman said darkly. "Tansy Norris, bless her soul, went to sleep last Saturday night and never woke up."

"She's dead!" I shared a stunned look with my friends.

"I'm sorry to say it's a fact. A fireman pulled her out, but smoke inhalation got her anyway." The woman lowered her gun, sadness replacing the suspicion on her weathered face. "Did you know her well?"

"Not exactly," I answered. "We're looking for her cousin, Jessica Hart."

"Never heard of her. I wasn't that close to Tansy. She kept to herself mostly."

"You don't remember meeting Ms. Hart, a woman who looked a bit like me?" Varina asked, touching her reddish hair. "It's very important we find her. Can't you help us?"

"The Lord helps those that helps themselves," she quoted briskly. "I am sorry, but ain't my concern."

"How did the fire happen?" I asked.

"The sheriff says it's an accident. That Tansy left a stove burner on." Reena shrugged. "But I don't buy it."

"Why not?" Chase and Varina asked at the same time.

"Tansy wasn't careless. But she did have at least one enemy." She tucked in a wisp of dark hair that had escaped from her cap. "There was this fellow visited her the morning of the fire, and they had words."

"They argued?" Eric questioned.

"They sure did. I couldn't hear what they said, but they sounded angry. And when that dark bald fellow left, he slammed her door so hard, the pictures on my shop walls rattled." She paused, running her tanned palm across her forehead. "Then that night, the Sailor's Delight burned down. Sure doesn't sound like an accident to me."

A *deliberate* accident, I thought ruefully. Then I remembered my two near-miss "accidents." Add the threatening note and the only accident was that I was still in one piece.

"Did the sheriff question the man?" Chase leaned forward.

"Not that I know of. No one knew who he was." Reena frowned. "But I do remember he had an accent."

"Like mine?" Eric asked.

"No. Maybe Spanish or Italian." She stepped over to a pile of charred wood and broken seashells, nudging them with the butt of her gun. Bending down, she picked up a dirty but perfect spiral pink seashell, which she tucked into her pocket.

"So you think he came back and set the fire?" I asked.

"Could be." She frowned. "But ain't nothing can be done without proof."

I shared a look with my friends, knowing we all suspected Dr. Victor. He was bald, he had an accent, and he wanted to find Dr. Hart.

Sadness filled me for Tansy. If only we'd been able to save her. But we were too late.

"You kids best be going." Reena's mouth narrowed to a thin line and she lifted her gun again. "No reason to stay around. Not unless you want to come next door and shop at my place."

I looked at the charred ruins of Sailor's Delight. Then I looked at the ominous rifle. "Shopping sounds like an excellent idea," I said quickly.

It came as no surprise to me that my friends all agreed.

A short time later, I was the proud owner of a nifty sand dollar night-light and organic seaweed shampoo. Varina had bought a seascape T-shirt and Eric was standing at the cash register, paying for a rubber fish-shaped toy for his dog. Chase didn't buy anything; instead he paced anxiously, like a wild creature in a cage. I noticed his hand cupping his ear, the way he often did when he was using his acute hearing.

Walking around a fishnet display of seashells and driftwood, I went over to him. "What's up?" I asked.

He put his finger to his lips, then tilted his head toward the back of the shop. "Something weird's going on here. I heard noises from behind that door. Someone's back there."

"But Reena said she ran her business alone."

"Exactly." Chase raised his dark brows. "Don't let on that we're suspicious, but tell Eric to come over here."

"So he can use his super eyesight?"

Chase nodded, and then I was moving; at a casual pace, pretending to browse around the shop, and yet quivering with anticipation.

I pasted a smile on my face as I went up to the cash register. "Hey, Eric. You gotta see this great seagull statue."

"I'm not into seagulls," he said as Reena rang up his purchase.

"You'll like these," I insisted, grabbing his arm and gripping it tightly. "Come on. Now."

"Go ahead, son," Reena said with an unsuspecting

grin. "Check it out. Could be you'll find something else to buy."

Eric's gaze met mine, and I gave him a sharp look. His black eyes widened and his expression grew alert. Message received. He quickly thanked Reena for his purchase, then followed me to the other side of the room, where Chase and Varina were conferring in low voices.

"I'm positive I heard something," Chase whispered. "But it's quiet back there now." He glanced up with relief when he saw Eric. "Help me out here, Eric."

"Sure. What can I do?"

"See that door in the back?"

"Yeah," Eric said with a nod. "It says 'Employees Only.' "

"Reena told us she ran her business alone, and yet I heard movement back there," Chase explained. "Could you use your vision to check it out?"

"Sure." Eric grinned, then reached up to remove his glasses in preparation for fixing his gaze on the door. "I'll give it a try."

With Eric's Enhance-X25 clone vision, he could see through solid objects as well as over a mile away. But without his glasses to steady him, his powerful eyesight threw off his equilibrium and turned him into a klutz, into someone more like Clark Kent than Superman. So I crossed my fingers and hoped he didn't stumble or break anything too expensive.

While Eric concentrated on the door, I glanced over at Reena, who was watching us from across the room. Her mouth was puckered with curiosity, and I could tell she was ready to come over and find out why we were whispering in a huddle.

I knew that more whispering would only add to her suspicions, so I moved away from my friends and pretended to admire a display of polished rocks and crystals.

"Gorgeous!" I exclaimed, loudly enough to get the

shopkeeper's attention. I picked up a multifaceted amethyst stone and held it high. "Reena, how much is this? It would look great as a necklace."

I imagined dollar signs sparkling from Reena's eyes as she rattled off an amount that seemed absurdly high. She eagerly reached over and found another amethyst stone and suggested I put them in earrings. While she raved about the stones, I snuck a glance at Eric.

Suddenly, his jaw dropped and he gasped loudly.

"I can't believe it!" he exclaimed. "She looks just like Varina!"

TWENTY-THREE

"Jessica Hart!" I exclaimed, the amethyst stone slipping from my fingers and clinking against the other polished stones.

"HEY!" Reena thundered. "What's going on?"

But Chase, Varina, and Eric were already bolting for the forbidden door. Chase reached it first, yanked it open, and disappeared inside.

"No one's allowed back there!" Reena screamed, nearly knocking over a wooden statue of a sailor. "STAY OUT!"

I ignored Reena and dodged past her, following my friends through the doorway. Reena continued to protest, but I was already in the room, taking in everything at a glance; a small studio apartment complete with kitchenette, living room, TV, and connecting bathroom. This wasn't a storage room. Someone had been living here— and that someone had just ducked out a back door into a rear parking lot.

"She's getting into a car!" Eric exclaimed.

"We have a car, too," Chase put in, all of us rushing

outside, everything happening so quickly my head spun.

"There she goes!" Eric shouted, pointing to a pale blue Saturn, its door slamming and engine firing up.

"Come on!" Chase shouted to us, heading for our car.

I didn't hesitate, racing over to the rear door of Professor Fergus's sedan and flinging myself inside. Eric piled in beside me. And up front, Varina reached for her seat belt as Chase started the motor and roared off in pursuit.

"Hold on," Chase warned us as he yanked the wheel to the right and increased his speed. Up ahead, the blue car sped away, the driver breaking all posted limits in her haste to escape.

Varina glanced toward the backseat, her lips pressed anxiously. "Eric, did she really look like me?"

"I think so, but older and more serious. Her dark red hair reminded me of yours, too. But she looked scared."

"Scared of us?" Varina guessed in surprise. "But why? We're just trying to help."

"Maybe she doesn't—," Chase started, then broke off when an enormous semitruck pulled out in front of him. He hit the brakes, slowing to a crawl as he yelled, "Hey! Move it, buddy!" But the truck only puffed black diesel smoke in reply. Chase swore under his breath, then jerked the wheel to the left, changing lanes and zooming past the truck.

"Good work," I told Chase.

"The blue car is still ahead," Eric pointed out. "But we're catching up. Faster, Chase!"

"My foot is to the floor already!"

"You're doing great," Varina said, reaching out to pat Chase's shoulder. "I just hope we can catch her . . . especially if she's my . . . Dr. Hart."

"If she is, then Reena was lying to us," I said angrily. "She knew where Jessica Hart was all along. Chase! The blue car just turned left on that side road."

"I'm there already. Sit tight and hold on."

Chase gripped the steering wheel, holding his breath as traffic zoomed by in the other direction, then swerving suddenly and slicing between swift cars. One car honked, but we were already racing down the narrow drive, away from the main road, toward open fields and a distant vista of clouds and ocean.

Where was the woman headed?

The terrain grew rougher, more hills and empty miles of grassy pasture. The blue car disappeared for a moment in the dip of a hill, then rose again to zoom farther ahead of us.

"She's getting away!" I cried, digging my fingers into the seat in front of me. "Come on, Chase! Hurry!"

Chase didn't reply, but in a flash of reflection from the rearview mirror, I saw the tense set of his jaw and the steel determination in his blue-gray eyes. If it was humanly possible to catch up to the fleeing car, Chase would do it.

"Check out that road up ahead!" he suddenly shouted. "I think we can cut her off by going that way."

I looked but saw only rolling hills, blowing yellow-green grasses, and several cows. There was a faint trail of crushed grass and rough dirt, but this "road" was more of a cattle trail: two rutted paths through high grasses that went downhill toward a distant paved road. It would be bumpy, full of ruts and rocky obstacles. I opened my mouth to argue against this "shortcut," but it was too late—we were already being jerked and jostled in our seats like floppy Beanie Babies.

Varina squealed, Eric groaned, and I summoned my strength, using it to hold tight so I didn't bounce through the roof. The road dipped and rose at awkward angles, tossing the sedan like a paper cup on a stormy ocean.

"We're almost there!" Chase called, turning sharply to avoid a huge puddle of water, but still hitting the edge of it and sending up a muddy spray that splattered the windows.

"Uncle Jim is going to freak when he sees his car," Varina moaned.

"Not if we bring Dr. Hart home," Eric said hopefully.

"If it's really her," I put in. I hadn't gotten a look at the woman, and found it hard to believe Varina's adult clone would run from us. Dr. Hart knew about Varina, even had some kind of mental contact, so why run away? It just didn't make sense.

As we left the dirt road, our car made a sharp left back onto the smooth highway. And the blue Saturn was only a few car lengths in front of us.

"Great luck!" Chase rejoiced. "There's a construction zone. She'll have to slow down, and then we'll have her."

"Way to go, Chase!" Varina yelled.

Leaning forward, I felt a surge of excitement. Orange construction cones appeared at the side of the road and there was a warning sign of bridge work ahead. Yes! We were gaining on the car, were practically bumper-to-bumper now. I could only see a vague shape of the driver, and wished we were close enough to see her face, to find out for myself if she truly resembled Varina.

On a narrow bridge up ahead, a flagwoman waved a sign signaling drivers to stop. Nearby, a monstrous crane hoisted a clam bucket high and then swiveled to drop dirt, branches, and clumps of soggy river debris into a waiting dump truck. The bulky dump truck backed up toward the entrance to the bridge, its noisy beeps warning people to stay away.

"We've got her—," Chase began, but broke off when the blue car kept on moving rather than slowing for the construction zone, striking several orange cones and sending them flying toward our car. One cone flew at our windshield, but Chase swerved to the right and missed it.

"She's crazy!" I shook my head in disbelief.

"Or desperate," Varina said solemnly.

Eric pointed. "She's still heading for the bridge."

"But the dump truck is blocking the bridge!" Varina gasped. "She'll be killed!"

My hands flew to my face as the blue car raced toward the rear of the dump truck. Despite the shouts of workers, the car didn't slow. The dump truck was moving slowly, seemingly unaware of the danger.

The blue car swerved suddenly to the left, narrowly missing the dump truck and nearly sideswiping a bridge rail. Then it sped over the bridge and disappeared on the other side.

Chase slowed, but impatiently tapped his fingers against the dash, and I caught a glimpse of grim determination in his gaze. "I can't give up now. Hold on! I'm going for the bridge!"

TWENTY-FOUR

"No, Chase!" Varina protested, touching his arm, her face wild with fear. "Don't do it!"

"But we'll lose her!"

"We've already lost her," Varina said sadly, her tone full of heartbreak and confusion. "Please, stop."

"Yeah," Eric agreed. "It's too risky."

"I guess you're right." Chase's shoulders sagged as he hit the brake, slowing for the construction. When the road was clear, he sighed and flipped a U-turn.

We didn't speak on the discouraging drive back to Sea Escapes. There wasn't much to say anyway. Instead of finding answers today, we'd only added more questions.

We could only hope Reena would answer a few of them.

But when we reached Sea Escapes, there were no cars in the parking lot and there was a big sign on the door. *Closed.*

On the long drive home, we discussed ideas and possibilities. The more we talked, the more confused we became. Why had the woman been hiding in the back room? Was she Dr. Hart or not? And what about Tansy's tragic death in the fire? Had Dr. Victor been responsible? But why kill Tansy when it was Dr. Hart he was after?

Way too many questions. No wonder my head ached by the time we reached the Fergus house. As I opened my car door, a breeze swept over me and I smelled the acrid whiff of the burnt building. The odor was clinging to my skin and hair.

Chase stepped out of the sedan, keys jingling from his fingers as he led the way into the house.

Professor Fergus met us in the entry and began asking how our trip had gone. There was a gleam of expectation in his gaze, and my heart sank knowing how upset he'd be when we told him about the burnt building and the fleeing woman who may have been his lost love.

Not having the stomach to watch this dear man's hopes get crushed, I left the explaining to the others and said I was going to bed early.

"Wait, Allison," the Professor said, reaching over to pick up a box from the coffee table. "This came by special delivery for you."

"Really?" I wasn't in the mood, but I *loved* gifts. Was it an early sweet-sixteen birthday present from my mother? Maybe she missed me after all.

But it wasn't from my adopted mother—it was from my genetic parent. Cressida Ray.

I waited until I reached the privacy of my room— taking Varina with me, of course—then ripped into the purple and silver wrapping.

"Ooh!" I cried with awe as I lifted a sheer, daisy-yellow, ankle-length slip with ivory overlay. There were matching high-heel sling-backs with dainty yellow bows, plus a gold rope necklace and funky flower-shaped gold earrings.

"Wow!" was all Varina could say.

"Cressida is like my fairy godmother."

"So try it on already, Cinderella," Varina said teasingly. "Go ahead."

I didn't need to be asked twice. Off came my overalls, and on slipped the sheer dress. I twirled in place, enjoying the soft brush of lace against my legs. Skipping over to my full-length mirror, I checked out this new look.

I found myself staring at someone I barely recognized. She glowed with self-assurance and confidence. The stranger in the mirror had my face and figure, but she was different, as if Cressida's essence had blended with mine.

"You look gorgeous," Varina said.

"Not exactly gorgeous, but not bad." I grinned, giving another small spin in front of the mirror. "Hey, I'm like a real model."

"Well, it's in your DNA."

"I never liked the whole idea of modeling." I stared into my dark eyes, seeing Cressida instead of myself. "But I never tried it. Maybe I was born to model."

"You were born to be yourself." Varina sat down on my bed beside the opened clothing box. "I think you need to make your own destiny."

"Maybe." But I wasn't so sure anymore—the urge to parade and pose in front of a camera was suddenly strong. Too bad I couldn't at least try it.

"Shouldn't you read the letter?" Varina asked, pointing to a long beige envelope at the bottom of the gift box.

I hadn't noticed the letter, but now I eagerly ripped into it and quickly read the short message.

Darling Allison,
Enjoy the "twin" outfit. I bought one for myself, too. Next time we go out, we'll really look alike.
    See you Thursday.
                                            Love, Cressida

I stared at the closing words. Of course, she didn't really love me—she barely knew me. But the more time we spent together, the more she'd realize that we were kindred souls.

Glancing up, I saw Varina staring at the beige envelope with an odd expression.

"Allison, you'd better look at this again." Varina scrunched her forehead and stared at the letter. "Where's the other letter you got today?"

"What letter?" I stopped cold, remembering the ugly threat I'd found in my locker. "Oh, *that*."

"Yeah. The 'Dead clones don't tell secrets' letter."

"In my pocket." I went to my overalls and reached into the back pocket and withdrew the crumpled envelope.

Varina studied the envelope and frowned. "I thought so."

"What?" I demanded.

"Look at the letter from Cressida and then look at the threatening letter," Varina said, placing them side by side on a dresser top.

The beige envelopes were similar. Scratch that—they were identical, down to the tiny gold design on the bottom. And the matching stationery was identical, too.

My heart nearly stopped, stunned by disbelief.

It couldn't be true, and yet there was no other explanation.

Both of the letters had been written on Cressida's stationery.

TWENTY-FIVE

Varina couldn't talk me out of it.

When I make up my mind about something, there's no turning back. And I'd made up my mind to spend the day with Cressida. I couldn't pass up this chance to learn more about my DNA double. I also wanted to find out who'd really sent the threatening letter. Certainly not Cressida. So who?

I wondered about this Thursday morning as I sat in a chair inside a portable trailer while Cressida's hairdresser, Shirley, fluffed and sprayed my hair. It was Cressida's idea to fix up my hair and makeup, and I'd said it would be okay. So I closed my eyes as hair spray misted around my face, its pungent odor nearly choking me.

So far, this makeover was not fun.

Shirley, a shapely woman with masses of freckles and a curly mop of maroon hair, worked quickly and quietly. By the time she finished, my hair was cascading in soft waves around my shoulders.

Next, she retrieved a makeup case from a cabinet and

began smoothing foundation cream onto my face. As she worked, I had the oddest feeling. Like I knew her. The freckles, kinky red hair, and small mouth were so familiar.

Then I realized why.

"Sarah Ann!" I snapped my fingers. "You're related to her, right?"

"Don't move," she grumbled, reaching for a tissue and wiping eye shadow from my cheek.

"You didn't answer me."

"I'm concentrating on my work, and I caution you to do so, too."

"Just tell me if you're related to Cressida's stepdaughter?"

"Of course I am." In the mirror, I saw her lips twist wryly. "Sarah Ann is my daughter."

"I knew it! But why do you work for Cressida? I mean, you were both married to Jackson. That has to be so weird."

"Do you always talk this much?" she asked sarcastically.

"No." I grinned. "Usually I talk even more, but I'm tired this morning. So how come you're working for Cressida?"

"She hired me. Simple as that." She set down a tube of lip gloss and shrugged. "Also, I do it for Sarah Ann."

"Why?"

"My daughter deserves a shot at modeling. Her father refuses to represent her, says she's not the right type, but I know better. Sarah Ann has star quality. You saw it, didn't you?"

"Uh, I guess." Actually, I didn't have a clue.

"My Sarah Ann is talented, and she deserves a chance at modeling. I'll do whatever it takes to help her."

There was a catch in her voice, and it tugged on my heart. What a devoted, loving mother. I wished then that my mother were like her. But my mother, ambitious and organized, bonded with her daily schedule, not her only daughter. I wondered if Sarah Ann knew how lucky she was.

That was all the conversation I could squeeze out of Shirley. Naturally, my thoughts drifted to the threatening letter. I didn't need Varina's super memory to recall the five dire words.

Dead clones don't tell secrets.

I'd originally thought Dr. Victor sent that letter, but now I wasn't so sure. He was dangerous, but he wanted to learn clone secrets, not keep me from telling them.

So who had sent the letter? And why had they used Cressida's stationery? Was it a deliberate attempt to cast suspicion on her?

"All done," Shirley stated, whipping the plastic drape from my shoulders.

I looked in the mirror and blinked at my transformation from gangly teen to glamorous temptress. With my lips shimmering peach, my cheekbones shadowed, and my dark eyes shaded dramatically, I looked even more like Cressida. The lines of time blurred and blended with the simple brush of makeup.

"You wait here and I'll go tell Cressida I'm done." Shirley rose and left the trailer.

As the door banged shut behind her, I swiveled in my chair and looked around the room. It was a combination living room, makeup studio, and office.

The office area called to me.

With a quick glance through the window to make sure no one was watching, I crossed the room and began snooping. The desk held a computer, printer, fax machine, and in/out basket. I wasn't a whiz like Eric, so I ignored the computer and opened desk drawers.

In the first one I found official-looking documents, paper clips, a stapler, Post-it notes, pens, a box of staples, and rubber bands. In the next drawer, I found more papers, and also a yummy stash of junk food: Milky Ways, Three Musketeers, and Kit Kats.

In the third drawer, I hit pay dirt. There were more papers, including a box of beige envelopes with matching stationery—the same paper and envelopes I'd received twice.

My head swam, and I leaned against the desk, taking deep cleansing breaths. *Proof.* Now I had positive proof that the threatening note had come from here. Still, I couldn't believe Cressida had anything to do with it. It had to be someone else with access to this trailer.

I glanced out the window at the many employees busily working on camera and outdoor lighting equipment, or the others who waited and talked in folding chairs. Most were strangers to me, but I recognized a few of them: Dolores, Jackson, Shirley, Sarah Ann, and of course Cressida.

One of them knew I was a clone. Cressida's clone. And one of them had set the dirt trap for me, which could have proven deadly if not for my strength. But why threaten and try to hurt me? It just didn't make sense.

Carefully shutting the desk drawers, I hurried back to my chair. And minutes later there was a tap on the door.

Sarah Ann peeked inside, pushing back her curly red hair. "Cressida's taking a break and wants to see you," she said.

Her expression was flat, and yet I sensed hostility in her. I wondered if she was my enemy. Had she found out I was a clone? Or was she simply jealous of my new relationship with Cressida? Jackson, her own father, raved about my appearance, wanting to hire me and ignoring her. Plenty of reason for resentment.

Or could Jackson have sent the threatening note? But why offer me a job if he didn't want me around? Unless it was a smoke screen to hide an ulterior motive. But what motive could he possibly have? And if he knew I was a clone, how had he found out?

Major paranoia alert.

If I didn't get my wild suspicions under control, I'd really lose it.

So I took a deep breath, then followed Sarah Ann across the park. As I walked, I admired the tranquil scenery. Fulton Park was a beautiful foothill location where fir, pine, and oak trees towered in shady greenness. There was a small zoo, picnic tables, and walking trails that wove through the woods down to a swift, sparkling river.

There was also a playground with swings, slides, and climbing bars. This area was roped off for the modeling shoot, and Cressida stood by the swings. She wore a white gauzy dress and her blond hair swirled angelically around her shoulders. When she saw me, she beckoned with a wave.

I waved back and headed toward her. As I crossed the grass, I had an uneasy sense of being watched.

Swiveling my head to look around, I didn't see anything unusual. Yet the prickly feeling persisted.

"Allison, you look lovely!" Cressida welcomed me with a hug. "I'm so glad you're here."

"Me too."

"As a surprise for you, I've persuaded one of the photographers to shoot a few pictures of us together. The pictures will be keepsakes of our meeting."

"As long as I don't have to actually model." I gave a shaky laugh. "Sitting still for a long time seems like hard work."

"No harder than rock climbing," she said with a teasing grin. "And you did that beautifully, like a real athlete. I was impressed and envious. Do you work out?"

"Not exactly." I pressed my lips together with amusement. "But I am pretty strong. You'd be surprised."

"I'm sure I would." She squeezed my hand fondly.

"Everything about you has been a wonderful surprise."

"There could be a few more surprises. But I'll tell you later, when we're completely alone."

"We should be able to leave after the shoot. And I won't let Dolores or Jackson interfere. We could either go back to my hotel or there's an outlet mall not far from here. Feel like shopping?"

"Always," I said teasingly. "My credit cards are itching for some action."

"Great." She grinned. "A girl after my own heart."

A man I didn't know called us over. Cressida explained that he was Raleigh, the "most talented photographer in the world."

A few minutes later, with hot lights blazing down on us, the photographer began to snap pictures. I felt stiff sitting beside Cressida, who posed artfully. I moved as gracefully as a robot on stilts. Even my smile felt stiff and unnatural.

Give me a hammer, nails, and some 4×4's anytime. If this was how it felt to be a model, I couldn't wait to head for a construction site.

And all the while I continued to have an eerie "someone's watching" feeling. When I mentioned it to Cressida, she just waved her hand and said that of course people were noticing me, given my "new look."

"Maybe." I sat on a swing beside her, digging my feet in the sand and glancing around uneasily. Intense lights shone down on us like miniature artificial suns.

She patted my hand, then reached up to smooth back a strand of my hair. "Relax and have fun."

"I am. It's cool to be here. Have you been modeling long?"

"Since I was seven. It's all I ever wanted to do."

"Really?" I gave her a surprised look. "You never tried anything else?"

"Not since I was ten or eleven. I loved paper dolls and started making my own line of clothing for them.

Dresses by Cress, I called it." She laughed, a faraway gleam in her dark eyes. "I planned to become a famous fashion designer."

"So why didn't you?"

"I already had a career. I was the White Delight toothpaste girl, and I also had a small part on a soap opera. Dolores had just started managing my career, and things were great. Sure, I've had ups and downs, but I've never stopped working." She smiled as she held out her hand to me. "And speaking of work, I've got to get busy. When I'm done, we'll talk more."

I nodded, then found a seat at a wooden picnic table. For a while, I just watched the busy activity. I noticed that Cressida did a lot of hurrying, then waiting. She might have been the star of the shoot, but she was receiving orders, not giving them.

When Cressida went to her trailer for a costume change, I stood up to stretch my legs for a while. I left the blare of artificial lights and wandered through the tangle of majestic trees, toward the clamor of animal noises from the nearby zoo.

It was a small zoo, not much bigger than my father's topiary garden, but certainly more interesting, with a fun assortment of wild animals. The plaques explained how most had been rescued after being injured, and now thrived in protected captivity.

Watching an elegant lion swish her tail as she curled up in the sunshine, I thought of Cressida. She was like a caged animal in a way, although the bars that imprisoned her were invisible. She lived in a pampered, protected world where people watched over her, admiringly but controllingly. She had everything she wanted and seemed happy, but was that enough? What about the little girl who created Dresses by Cress? Was she happy?

I sighed, deposited a generous donation in the zoo's money box, then wandered back into the park. I could see the bright lights and camera flashes through the trees, and realized Cressida was working again.

As I walked through the park, the hair on the back of my neck tingled and I felt sure someone was watching. I also heard a muffled footstep behind me.

When I stopped and whirled around, I was facing a middle-aged woman with a mountain of velvet-black hair piled on her head. And she was holding something in her hands—aimed right at me!

TWENTY-SIX

"Hold it right there!" the woman ordered, lifting the camera and assaulting me with blinding flashes. Click, click, click. Her camera whirled.

"HEY!" I covered my face with my hands and backed away. "What are you doing?"

"My job. Come on, give me a nice smile."

"NO! Stop it!"

"Sure. Whatever you say." The camera lowered, and I noticed that the woman's blue eyes were highlighted with garish blue, purple, and silver makeup. She moved toward me, her gaze as predatory as a hungry wolf's. "Just answer a few questions and then I'll leave. What's your name? Where'd Cressida find you? Are you her illegitimate child?"

"What?" I cried, bewildered. "Who are you?"

"Dominique Eszlinger with *EXPOSED!*" As if by magic she pulled out a small tape recorder and waved it in my face. "How long have you known Cressida?" she demanded. "Are you a model? Is that really your face or is it the result of plastic surgery?"

"You're crazy!"

"Just answer my questions. What's your connection with—"

"ENOUGH!" a voice interrupted. "Shut up, Dominique."

I turned and saw a very angry Cressida Ray. She swept past me and glared at Dominique. "You are *not* welcome here. So please leave."

"Not until I get a scoop. Is she your daughter?"

"Don't be ridiculous!" Cressida's laugh was sharp and tinged with fury. "You've been hounding me ever since we were teenagers and I beat you out of the Barky Beagle commercial. Get over it already. If I'd been pregnant, you would have known."

"So who is this girl?" Dominique persisted, her ice-blue eyes narrow and suspicious. "What's the dirt on her?"

"The only dirt is in your mind, Dominique. And to scoop all that dirt, you'd need a garbage truck." Cressida smiled as Jackson and a few other men came up beside her. "Now please leave or my friends will be forced to escort you off this shoot."

Dominique glared daggers, then whirled around and stomped off. I let out the deep breath I'd been holding.

"Wow," I murmured to Cressida. "What just happened?"

"Nothing important," she replied, but I noticed that her hands were shaking.

Jackson put his arm around Cressida. "Don't let Dominique get to you, Cressy."

"I can't help it. She's like a germ, and I'm so sick of her following me around."

"Forget about her. I'll tell you what: We'll break for lunch and everyone can relax. How's that sound?"

"Thanks, Jackson," she said warmly. "That'd be great."

I watched the interaction between the two and sensed

they shared something deeper than a business relationship. So why had they gotten a divorce? Jackson was kind of old, but a real hottie. And Cressida's voice got all soft when she spoke to him.

I wanted to ask Cressida these questions and more, but Dolores rushed over and insisted that Cressida rest in the trailer. With her entourage closing in, I was left alone. That was fine. I'd always rather be on my own than have a bunch of people tell me what to do.

After eating a sandwich, chips, and an apple from the food table, I decided to go for a walk. Since I'd already been to the zoo, I opted for the opposite direction this time, down the woodsy path toward the river.

Birds chirped and fluttered on high branches and I caught a glimpse of a gray squirrel skittering up a tree trunk. The loud rush of water increased as I traveled closer to the river. I trudged down a steep, narrow trail, and found a lovely cascading waterfall tucked into a rock wall; a gift from Mother Nature wrapped in bushes and craggy sandstone. My breath caught in delight, and I stopped to stare.

The torrent of tumbling water captured me, showering me with a sense of peace and contentment.

"Nature's awesome, huh?" someone said.

"What!" Nearly jumping out of my skin, I whirled around. "Chase! What are you doing here?"

He grinned. "Nice day for a hike in the woods."

"You've been spying on me!"

"I wasn't the only one. I saw that snoopy reporter and heard what went down."

"So why didn't you warn me Dominique was watching?"

"She seemed harmless. I'm more concerned with making sure that jerk who sent you the threatening letter doesn't hurt you."

"Did Professor Fergus tell you to follow me?"

"No, it was my idea. But when I told him, he was relieved."

I thought of how Jackson and Dolores overprotected Cressida, and I bristled. "I do not need a bodyguard."

"You got one anyway."

"Forget it." My hand brushed against a branch, which I snapped in two. "If this were made of steel, I'd still be able to break it. Does that sound like someone who needs a protector?"

"Strength can't protect you from everything. You didn't even hear me, and I've been following you all day." He cupped his hand to his ear and added, "I can eavesdrop on conversations a mile away and I can—"

He stopped suddenly, his eyes widening, then he grabbed my shoulders and shoved me to the ground. "Get down!" he shouted.

The world rushed by in a blur. I heard a pop as I crashed onto dirt, rocks, and weeds. My head spun, my heart thundered, and I had no idea what was going on.

"Chase!" I cried from my squashed position on the ground. "What's happening?"

He didn't answer. Instead he jumped to his feet and took off running up the steep, wooded hillside.

"What in the world?" I muttered as I sat up slowly and brushed dirt and leaves out of my hair. My nylons were snagged and the delicate gauzy dress was a mess. Oh, no! How was I going to explain this to Cressida? I told myself that Chase better have a good explanation for having thrown me to the ground.

I stood up and peered through the dense foliage.

So where was he?

Just when I'd decided to go after him, Chase returned. His face was flushed and his forehead glistened with sweat. "Damn. I lost him."

"Him?"

"Or maybe her. Eric's the one with the super eyesight, not me. But thank goodness for my hearing." He gently touched my arm and peered into my face. "You're all right, aren't you?"

"Sure. Why wouldn't I be?"

"You don't know?" His dark brows arched with surprise. Then he walked over to where we'd been standing when he'd pushed me to the ground. After looking around, he crossed over to a massive sandstone rock.

"Check this out," he said in a grim voice. He pointed to a dark spot on the sandstone.

Stepping to the rock, I realized the dark spot was a small round hole. Peering closer, I could see the shadow of something wedged inside the hole. A small pebble. No, not a pebble.

"A bullet!" I gasped, sagging back into Chase's sturdy arms. "That popping sound—it was a gunshot! Someone shot at us!"

"No, not us." Chase met my gaze and added ominously, "You. Someone tried to kill you."

TWENTY-SEVEN

"**Y**ou're shaking," Chase said gently. "And your hair and clothes are messy. I'm sorry I pushed you so hard."

"Well, I'm not sorry." I managed a feeble smile. "You saved my life. Thanks. But how did you know?"

"I heard the gun as it fired. You were standing right in front of this rock. If you hadn't moved, the bullet would have hit your head."

"Ouch." I touched my head, shivering. "It's so incredible. Someone really tried to kill me. And this time I can't pretend it's an accident."

"Wait a minute." Chase narrowed his gaze at me. "What do you mean 'this time'?"

Oops. Hadn't meant to let that slip. Now I'd have to tell Chase everything and I'd be stuck with a bodyguard for life. But since it was my life that was at stake, maybe a bodyguard wasn't such a bad idea.

With an uneasy glance at the hole in the rock, I told Chase everything, about the falling roof shakes and my imprisonment in the dirt hole. Add the threatening note, and it was obvious someone was out to get me.

"So what now?" I asked Chase. "Call the police?"

"Can't risk that. Then we'd have to show them the threatening letter and explain we were clones." Chase shook his head. "We're on our own here. Too bad the bullet is stuck in the rock. It might be good evidence for later."

"You want it? No problem." I couldn't resist a low chuckle. Then I placed both of my hands on the rock and concentrated on summoning my strength.

With the bullet hole between my palms, I pressed hard, forcing the rock to crack. Pieces of the boulder started crumbling away, until finally the bullet fell from the opening and I quickly caught it in my palm. Small, hard, and twisted. To think this tiny pebblelike metal could have ended my life.

"You're amazing." Chase grinned as I handed him the bullet. Then he tucked it into his shirt pocket. "Cool stunt. But you should have told us about the other stuff that happened to you."

"I guess."

"Why didn't you?" Chase asked as we slowly followed the path back to the park.

"Varina and Eric know about the roof shakes. But things have been so hectic since Dr. Victor threatened the Professor. The search for Dr. Hart has made things even crazier. And I didn't want to sound paranoid." I reached up to push aside a low-hanging branch. "I hoped I was just accident-prone."

"A concrete slab accidentally trapped you in a hole?" he asked skeptically.

"It seemed more logical than someone deliberately trying to kill me, at least until I found the letter in my locker." I shuddered. "Who do you think shot at me?"

"I'd like to blame Dr. Victor, but if he was going to

shoot at anyone, it'd be me. I'm the one with killer genes."

"So maybe he's a bad shot."

"Could be." Chase shrugged. "But it doesn't feel right."

"I know what you mean." I thought back to my chilling phone conversation. "When I talked to him on the phone, he was more focused on getting the Enhance-X25 formula. He didn't sound interested in me, and I'm sure he didn't send the letter." I quickly explained about finding the matching stationery in Cressida's trailer.

"Cressida's stationery?"

"Yeah, but don't blame her. A lot of people have access to the trailer. Cressida would never hurt me. Someone else did it."

"This is too weird." Chase frowned. "If only I'd been able to catch the shooter. But that jerk is long gone by now."

"Or nearby pretending that nothing unusual has happened and hanging out at the photo shoot," I said with a shiver.

We crested the hill by a rest room, and I went over to take a sip from an outdoor water faucet.

Chase took a sip also, his brow furrowed in concentration, then he gave me a deep look. "It's too dangerous for you to stay here. Come home with me."

"No way!" I pursed my lips stubbornly. "I promised Cressida I'd go shopping with her later."

"Wake up, Allison. Your life is in danger. How many accidents can you survive? Someone is still out there with a gun."

"I'm not running scared." I folded my arms across my chest. "The shooter won't try again today. I don't want to let Cressida down."

"Even if she's trying to kill you?"

"She isn't. Don't talk about her that way. She's like

my sister or my mother. And she'd never hurt me. We're too much alike."

"Just because you share DNA?" he demanded in a low, chilling tone. An angry flush darkened Chase's eyes to a steel gray. "If you go by that logic, then I'm a killer because of my DNA."

"It's not the same," I argued. "You wouldn't hurt anyone."

"Can you be sure?" he tossed back.

I didn't know what to say, so I closed my mouth and walked toward the playground. Chase walked with me, but neither one of us spoke.

When we reached the playground, I saw the lighting equipment and cameras standing idle. A few of the crew sat in folding chairs sipping sodas and eating lunch. But Cressida and her entourage weren't there. I figured they must be in the trailer, so I headed for the nearby parking lot.

Chase stayed with me, his expression sullen and distant. I could tell he was annoyed, but he still seemed determined to play out his role of bodyguard.

As we reached the trailer steps, Chase stopped and motioned for me to stop, too. He tilted his head in that way he did when he was using his super hearing. I knew he was listening to something I couldn't even begin to hear.

"What is it?" I asked.

"Shhsh!" He put his finger to his lips. "Your model and that bossy manager of hers are talking."

"So what?"

"They're talking about you."

"What are they saying?"

He cupped his hand to his ear. "The manager—"

"Dolores," I put in.

"Dolores just said, 'You're obsessed with that girl and it's not healthy. Stay away from her.' And your model replied, 'I'll do whatever I want. Stop treating me like a child.' "

"Good for Cressida," I murmured, glad she was showing some spirit. "What else?"

"Dolores said, 'You better take care of your health. Remember what the doctors said.' Cressida replied, 'What do doctors know? They predicted my heart would give out years ago. But I'm still here.' " Chase paused, then continued, "Now Dolores is angry. She said, 'Don't be childish! You're growing weaker every day.' "

"I already know about her bad heart," I confided to Chase. "But she's not sick or anything. Just fragile."

"Sounds more serious than that," Chase said, his head still tilted in listening mode. "Dolores is saying—" His eyes widened and he gave a sharp gasp.

He stood up swiftly and grabbed my hand. "I've heard enough. You're getting out of here."

"No." I jerked my hand away. "I've got a job to finish."

"You cannot stay around these people."

"Why?" I demanded. "I can't just leave."

"You have to. I think I know why someone tried to kill you."

"W-why?"

"Because you're Cressida's clone." He lifted his hand and pointed ominously at me. "And your genetic double needs a new heart."

TWENTY-EIGHT

It couldn't be true.

I mean, you didn't just rip out someone's heart and plop it into another person's body. Medical science was more complex than that. There were waiting lists, medications, and the threat of organ rejection. Recycling body parts required doctor consultation and careful preparation. Very complicated.

But cloning was complicated, too, and yet here I was.

It was hard to ignore the facts. Chase had overheard Dolores tell Cressida that a new heart would solve all their problems. Add that to the attempts on my life and the threatening note, and I didn't blame Chase for jumping to conclusions.

But would Dolores go as far as murder to save her employer?

It was weird to think anyone would try to kill me for my heart. That was something out of a sci-fi movie, not real life.

Yet in a warped way it made sense. Cressida needed a new heart, and who better than her own clone to provide a compatible organ? Someone had discovered why I looked so much like Cressida, and now this someone—probably Dolores—wanted to dissect me like a lab specimen for replacement body parts.

Major sick-puppy alert.

Okay, I admit it. I was freaked out, and my first impulse was to run away. Far, far away. But I couldn't take off without talking to Cressida first. A real bond had been growing between us, and I didn't want to hurt her.

So I refused to leave.

I folded my arms across my chest and stood up to Chase. Anger steamed from him like smoke puffing from a volcano before it blows. But instead of erupting, he just glared at me and swore under his breath. Then he turned and strode off, vanishing into a thick tangle of trees. I had a feeling he wasn't far away, though, and was watching me from a discreet distance.

A short time later, I went to sit at a picnic table and watch Cressida. She was posing on a playground swing and leaning backwards with her feet inches off the ground while people tugged on her hair, fixed her makeup, and ordered her around.

My mind whirled, and I wondered: Which of the "friendly" faces around Cressida wanted me dead?

Dolores, of course, was the prime suspect. She fussed over Cressida like a parent; she was far more devoted than the average employee. But could her devotion extend to murder?

And Jackson. He was both an employee and a former spouse. Double the motive. As he stood off to the side watching Cressida, his gaze lingered on her fondly. He still loved her, I was sure of it. But would he kill to keep her alive?

My head ached and I felt chilled. For the rest of the afternoon, I watched everyone with dark suspicions, from the photographer to Sarah Ann. Over and over the question raced through my mind: Which one of you tried to kill me?

By the time the crew shut down for the day, I was mentally exhausted. Cressida looked weary, too. She was awfully pale. Her condition scared me. And I felt a jolt of fear.

Had I found my soul mate only to lose her? Was a transplant her only chance at survival? And if she didn't get one, how much time did she have?

It was no surprise when she canceled our shopping plans.

"Sorry," Cressida said, glancing down as she fidgeted with her hands. "But I'm wiped out and can barely stand up. I need to rest. Maybe we can do something tomorrow."

"Bungee jumping?" I teased to hide my mixed feelings.

"Sure. But you jump first," she said with a half-smile. "Seriously, I enjoy having you here. It's so easy to be around you, and I know you aren't interested in modeling, but you should give it a chance. I think you'd be a natural."

"And the lie detector jumps off the scale," I teased.

"No. Really. The shots we took earlier will come out wonderful. Just you wait."

Shots. The word made me cringe, remembering the twisted metal I'd pulled from the rock. That bullet could have blown my brains out—though my heart might have lived on in a new body.

I would have gone home in Cressida's limo, but Chase reappeared and offered to drive me. He told Cressida a lame story about being in the area and stopping by to support me.

On the way home, Chase didn't say much and I knew he was still ticked off at me. I was too tired to care, and simply closed my eyes. When I opened them, we were pulling into the Fergus driveway.

"Thanks for being there for me today," I told Chase as I unfastened my seat belt.

He just shrugged as he shut the engine off.

"I mean it. You really saved my butt."

"You mean, your heart," he said, but his expression was friendlier and I could tell he wasn't mad anymore.

As I stepped out of the car, I mentally rehearsed telling Eric, Varina, and her uncle about the attempts on my life. I didn't want to just blurt it out, so maybe I'd start with the construction site accident, since they already knew about that, and work up to the shooting.

It was almost dark, and there were several lights on inside the two-story house. I glimpsed movement in the kitchen, and recognized Varina's reddish hair.

"There's Varina," I said pointing to the lit window as we left the car. "You should go talk to her."

"Why?"

"So you can work things out. She wanted to ask you to go somewhere with her, but she was upset when you defended Sandee."

"She doesn't even know Sandee."

"But she knows you," I pointed out. "And maybe . . . just maybe . . . she's afraid you have feelings for Sandee. Do you?"

"Of course not. Besides, I've got killer genes to deal with. I wouldn't wish myself on any decent girl." He gave me a dark look, then walked ahead and headed downstairs to his room.

Feeling like I'd really blown it, I went into the kitchen. Varina stood at the counter slicing vegetables for a salad.

"Allison. I was wondering when you'd get home."

"Well, I'm here, but I'm tired. I just want go to my room and rest until dinner. It's been a long day."

"Did you have fun?"

"Sort of," I admitted. "Modeling isn't something I'd want to do, but it was fun to watch. It would have been more fun if someone hadn't tried to kill me."

"WHAT?" Varina dropped the carrot she'd been slicing.

And then I told her.

"How terrifying!" she exclaimed when I'd finished. "I remember how scared I was when Dr. Victor aimed a gun at me. Thank goodness Chase was there to help you."

"Yeah. He's a great guy." Except for his moodiness, I almost added.

"I think about Chase way more than I should. I only wish I knew where I stood with him," she said with a wistful sigh. "When you guys were together, did he say anything about me?"

I hesitated, glancing into her gentle green eyes and struggling between truth and lies. Being honest was the right thing to do, but I couldn't bear to shatter Varina's hopes.

So I told her that Chase hadn't mentioned her.

The truth could wait for later.

For now, lies were safer.

TWENTY-NINE

Before Varina could ask me more questions, I heard the door open and voices pour in.

"Sounds like Eric's back," Varina said, dropping carrots in a salad bowl and turning away from the kitchen counter. "He and Starr had a dinner date."

"So that's where he's been. Geez, the things I miss by skipping school."

Varina unlocked the door and grinned. "I want to hear how things are progressing between the lovebirds."

"Me too," I agreed, following her down the hall. It still amazed me that serious Eric was going out with wild and popular Starr. I hoped she wouldn't end up hurting him.

But when I stepped into the foyer and saw the lip-lock Eric and Starr were sharing, it didn't look like anyone was being hurt.

Varina giggled, and I cleared my throat.

Startled, Eric jumped back, bumping his head against the partially open front door. "Uh, hi!" he said quickly, his dark skin blushing crimson. "I, uh, didn't see you guys."

"Wonder why," I teased.

"Guess it's time to go." Starr grinned, clearly enjoying herself. Her dangling moon-shaped earrings swayed, almost brushing her embroidered denim vest. She wore snug navy-blue jeans and a low-cut purple shirt that molded to her curvy figure. She reached out and gave Eric a kiss on the cheek. "See ya at school tomorrow."

Eric nodded, staring at her in a daze. Then he turned to me, and seemed to notice my serious expression. "Everything okay?"

"Well . . ." I paused to take a deep breath. "I'll tell you guys everything later, when Professor Fergus gets home. That way I won't have to repeat myself."

"Sure," Varina agreed.

"I hate being kept in suspense," Eric complained, but he didn't argue.

As soon as the Professor arrived home, we all gathered quietly in his office. "So what's this about? Have you heard from Jessica?"

"Nope," Chase said. "And when I tried calling Reena at Sea Escapes the phone just rang and rang. She's avoiding us."

"Then I'll go down there personally and demand the truth," the Professor said angrily. "I have to know what happened to Jessica. If she's in trouble, I want to help."

"We'll find out," Varina promised.

Eric suddenly stood up. "Uncle Jim, I just thought of another angle to check out. Mind if I use your computer?"

"Be my guest," the Professor said with a nod at his desk.

Eric crossed the room, then flipped on the computer and quickly went to work.

"Didn't you have something to discuss, Allison?" Chase asked purposefully.

"I guess," I said reluctantly. Then, taking a deep

breath, I told about the trip to the Rock Climbing Castle and the shooting incident in the park.

"Someone tried to kill you not once but *twice*?" Eric exclaimed when I'd finished.

"Probably." I nodded, glancing away uneasily.

Varina frowned. "Or maybe three times, if you count the roof shake incident."

"Yeah." Eric gave me a deep look. "You should have told us all of this earlier."

"I'm telling you now."

Eric frowned at me from over at the computer. "You could have been killed."

"But I'm fine," I tried to explain. "I didn't want you to worry."

"Well, FYI: We're worried," Eric said sharply. "You're the one who said we're 'clone cousins,' and yet you don't trust us with the truth."

"Allison, this is extremely serious." The Professor leaned forward on his desk, his forehead puckering with concern. "I knew Dr. Victor was dangerous, but he only seemed interested in the formula. I'm shocked that he's targeting you."

"But it's not him." I twisted the ends of my hair and explained about finding the matching stationery in Cressida's trailer. "It was someone who works for Cressida."

"Then you have to stay away from her," the Professor said, rubbing the scar over his brow.

"No! It's only one more morning, and I'll be surrounded by people all the time. Please, let me go."

"It's out of the question," Professor Fergus insisted.

"But if I don't go, they'll wonder why and ask awkward questions."

"Maybe she should go," Chase said. "I'll stay close and watch out for her. By snooping around and listening to conversations, I might be able to figure out what's going on."

"You really think so?" Professor Fergus asked doubt-fully.

"It's worth a try." Chase nodded. "We're *all* in danger if someone else knows about the cloning experiment. Maybe I can learn something important."

"All right. But be careful." Professor Fergus gave me a grave look, his hands shaking slightly. "Both of you. I only wish you hadn't waited so long to let us know what was going on. I'm disappointed in you, Allison. There are to be no more secrets. Understand?"

"Yeah." I nodded numbly, feeling like I'd let my friends down. And I had. Eric turned back to the computer, and I sensed his disappointment in me. Varina looked troubled, too.

For a moment, the only noise in the room was the soft tapping of Eric's fingers on the keyboard. Then suddenly he let out a whoop and exclaimed, "Hey, I found something!"

"What?" Professor Fergus asked.

"Information on Tansy Norris and the fire." Eric paused and added, "And it explains why Reena Bond lied to us."

THIRTY

"W hy would Reena lie?" Varina asked.

"To protect someone," Eric answered. He went on to explain how on a hunch he'd checked out Reena Bond. But he'd found nothing, no business or personal trail. Unusual. So he'd checked her business, Sea Escapes.

"And guess who owns it?" Eric gestured excitedly with his hands. "Tansy I. Norris."

"But she died in the fire," I pointed out.

"Nope." Eric shook his head. "Reena made up that story to throw us off track. Reena is a nickname for Irene—as in Tansy *Irene* Norris."

"Reena is Tansy?" Professor Fergus rubbed his beard, his brows knit together anxiously. "No wonder she was hiding Jessica. But that still doesn't explain why Jessica ran from you kids. I have to go there and talk to Reena."

"She'll just lie some more," Chase said.

"We'll make her tell the truth," Varina declared.

"And I'll be there to help this time," Professor Fergus said. "I'm giving exams tomorrow, but I'm free on Saturday. We can go then."

Varina, Eric, and Chase nodded agreement.

"Me too," I put in. "I had planned to volunteer at the construction site, but I can do that another day. I'd rather help you guys."

Eric gave me a skeptical look. "Don't do us any favors."

"I want to go."

He shrugged. Then Professor Fergus went on to discuss the trip. I was sitting among my friends, yet I had an uneasy sense of being left out. I could tell that Eric still resented me for keeping secrets, and I didn't blame him.

Eric's fingers flew across the computer keyboard. He gave a low whistle and announced he'd found a newspaper article on the Sailor's Delight fire. The fire was listed as a probable arson, with structural damage but no lives lost.

Tansy/Reena had purposely misled us.

That night I dreamed about fire, felt hot flames surround me and heard angry voices accusing me of lying. Hurt and fear swirled with the flames as I faced a crowd of faceless accusers. *But I didn't do anything wrong,* I tried to explain. Only no one could hear me.

It was a relief to open my eyes and realize I was safe in my own bed. Even better, I didn't have to go to school today. And despite the possible danger, I couldn't wait to see Cressida.

A few hours later, I sat in the trailer while Cressida was expertly made up by Shirley. I reclined nearby on a couch, flipping through a magazine and sipping iced tea. I noticed that even with heavy makeup on, Cressida looked unusually pale.

"You feeling okay?" I asked her.

"Sure. Although I'm half-asleep." Cressida closed her eyes as Shirley squirted on some hair spray. "I'm not a morning person."

"Me either. I'm always running late. Don't even ask me how many tardy slips I've gotten."

"I won't." She smiled. "As long as you don't ask how often I've made photographers wait for me. I'd probably be late everywhere if I didn't have such a prompt chauffeur. Fortunately, Leo is very disciplined and organized. I'm so used to his taking care of me, I don't even have a driver's license."

"You don't?" I set my magazine down. "I'm dying to get mine. Then I can apply to a construction apprenticeship program. That's my dream job."

"Construction?" Cressida repeated with disgust.

I saw Shirley's eyes widen, too. I smiled, enjoying their surprise. People were often startled by my career choice.

"I like hard work," I explained, then went on to describe the joy of building houses for needy people. Having goals made me feel good, and my voice rose with enthusiasm.

"But why choose such a strenuous occupation?" Cressida said. "Wouldn't you rather do something fun?"

"Construction *is* fun. I love the challenge of starting with practically nothing except basic materials, and watching a building grow."

"But you'll get splinters and calluses. And sun exposure is bad for your skin. Aim for something with excellent pay and working conditions."

"Like modeling?" I guessed with amusement.

"Why not? It's been great for me." Then she launched into a vivid description of her thrilling job perks: trips to Europe, Caribbean cruises, runway shows for royalty, and admiring fans. It did sound glamorous, and for a moment I was swept away in the fantasy of gliding down a Paris runway, cameras flashing and fans applauding.

I had to admit, it was a dazzling image.

Shirley announced she was finished, and Cressida stood up and studied herself in the mirror. Her blond hair was swept up in glittering combs, with only a few escaped curly tendrils to frame her face. She wore a flowing turquoise dress made of a light, crinkly material that whispered like the wind as she moved.

For a moment, I saw myself standing there. Older, mature, sophisticated. A transformation from the girl in overalls who hammered nails and smelled like sawdust. And I wondered who I really was—what kind of woman I'd grow to be.

The modeling shoot proceeded smoothly. I sat on a nearby bench and watched intently. Although I had brought the magazine along to help pass the time, I never glanced at it once. I was totally captivated by my clone's skill and elegance. When the shoot ended and the camera stopped flashing, I felt disappointed.

Done. All over. Farewell glamour, hello reality.

Now Cressida would drive away, board a plane, and fly out of my life. I'd miss her.

I went back to the trailer and waited for Cressida to join me. Minutes later, the door opened and she peeked inside.

"Are you alone?" she said with a furtive glance over her shoulder as she shut the door.

"Yeah. What's up?" I twisted my hair into a ponytail and wrapped a scrunchie around it.

"We don't have much time. Dolores isn't far behind." Her voice was low and hushed. "She's such a mother hen, she'll never approve of my idea."

"So what? Stop letting her push you around."

"That's just her way, and I don't mind most of the time. But since she caught me rock climbing, she's been worse than ever. She's thinks you're a bad influence."

"Me? No way!"

"I told her she was ridiculous, but she only hears what she wants to her. So I figured out a way to see you again before I leave town."

"Really?" I asked hopefully.

"You bet." Her dark eyes sparkled with mischief. "First I'll return to my hotel to pack. Then I'll say I'm too exhausted to go out to dinner and would rather have room service. Dolores won't want to leave, but I'll insist she go out to dinner with Jackson and Sarah Ann to celebrate a successful shoot."

I leaned against a counter and gave her a puzzled look. "How do I fit in?"

"My chauffeur will pick you up and bring you to the hotel, and then we'll have a private visit with no interruptions."

"But why do you have to sneak around?" I frowned. "If you want to see me, tell Dolores and Jackson to back off."

"Oh, I couldn't. It would seem ungrateful after all they've done for me. They take care of everything for me, make my life comfortable."

"Or like a cage," I murmured.

But she had turned toward the window and didn't seem to hear me. "Dolores is coming. Promise you'll meet me later."

"What if I can't get away?"

"You have to. There's a reason we have to talk alone."

"There is?" My heart jumped. "What?"

"It's too complicated to go into now. But it concerns your future. Please come."

"Well . . ." I bit my lip and hesitated. I was dying to hear what Cressida had to say. But I knew I should get permission from Professor Fergus first. Curiosity versus common sense.

Curiosity won. I whispered, "Okay," and nodded just as the door opened and Dolores strode inside.

"Cressida, why aren't you resting? You'll end up in the hospital if you don't take better care of yourself."

"I was just going to lie down," Cressida said with a sly wink at me before she went over to the couch.

The manager turned her attention to me. "Allison, are

you ready to go? The limo is waiting for you."

"I guess." I turned to Cressida and waved good-bye. I almost said, "See you later," but held my tongue.

Outside, I saw the limo idling in the parking lot. Instead of heading for it, I hesitated and glanced around for a red truck. Where was Chase? I knew he'd been here today watching out for me. But I didn't see him or his truck.

Heading for the limo, I stopped when I heard a familiar motor. Then the red truck appeared, turning the corner of the parking lot. Chase rolled down the window and waved me over.

I hurriedly called out to Leo that I wouldn't need a ride home, then joined Chase.

"Thanks," I told him as I slipped inside the truck. "Were you totally bored waiting for me?"

"Yes and no."

"What do you mean?"

"Waiting was dull. You were just sitting around for hours doing nothing."

"Hey, that 'nothing' was fun."

"This coming from the all-powerful girl who would rather smack nails than wear nylons." He gave me a surprised look. "Am I talking to the REAL Allison Beaumont?"

"Nope. I'm her clone," I teased.

"Not funny," he said, but I noticed he was grinning. He hit the gas and left the parking lot.

"So were you totally bored out of your mind or did you hear anything interesting?" I asked him.

"Some juicy stuff." His gray-blue eyes twinkled. "A photographer was hitting on a girl in a snug miniskirt— until he got a cell call from his wife."

"Ouch."

"And another guy was griping to a friend about his tight underwear."

"Double ouch." I chuckled. "Anything else?"

"Yup. That red-haired girl, Sarah Ann, told her mother she'd found a talent agent to represent her."

"Sarah Ann has an agent? That's great! But her father must be steaming." I grinned. "Jackson didn't take Sarah Ann's ambitions seriously. I'll bet he's sorry now."

"Could be." Chase checked his rearview mirror, then changed lanes. "And I heard something else. Only I'm not sure how to tell you."

"Why?"

"Dolores got a call on her cell phone. She whispered something about it being a bad time to talk, then went into the trailer and locked the door." He slowed for a yield sign. "Of course, I could still hear every word."

"Who called?"

"That snoopy reporter."

"Dominique Eszlinger?"

"Yeah." He nodded. "Dolores told the reporter she had a hot scoop. She said she could prove that Cressida has a daughter." He gave me a deep look. *"You."*

THIRTY-ONE

"No way!" I exclaimed. "Why would Dolores give false information to the Mudslinger?"

"She wasn't *giving* information." Chase paused. "She was *selling* it. And for a major amount."

"That's so low. I can't believe she'd betray Cressida." I turned my head and looked out the window at the blur of passing fields and housing developments. I considered the possibility that Cressida really was my mother. Had Professor Fergus been wrong about me? Maybe it was some other girl who'd been cloned in a floating laboratory. But then where had I gotten my incredible strength? And what about the scar on my ankle in the same place Eric, Varina, and Chase had clone tattoos?

I sighed. No matter how much I wanted Cressida for a mother, I knew it wasn't true.

So what was Dolores's game?

Shifting in the passenger seat, I asked Chase, "What else did you hear?"

"After the reporter agreed to pay megabucks, Dolores explained that Cressida hadn't physically given birth, that she didn't even know she had a child."

"So how can I be her daughter?" A frightening thought struck me. "Unless they found out about the cloning experiment."

"No, that's not it. Seventeen years ago Cressida had some eggs frozen at a fertility clinic. She wanted to make sure she could have kids after her career ended. Only someone broke into the clinic and stole her eggs. Dolores thinks they were sold on the black market." Chase's tone lowered. "And she said you're the result of one of those missing eggs."

"That's ridiculous!"

"Is it?" Chase asked, driving into the tree-lined subdivision we lived in. "Don't you ever wonder how Dr. Victor got the DNA to create us? He couldn't just ask for it. He probably hired someone to steal for him."

Chase's words sunk in, coming into focus with crystal clarity. He was right. But why would Dolores sell this very private information to the Mudslinger? Was her devotion to Cressida all an act? Or maybe there was a more sinister reason. If it were publicly revealed that I was related to Cressida, then, when I had an "unfortunate accident," it would be only logical to transfer my heart to Cressida's.

I put my hand on my chest, feeling the reassuring beats within. I was a person—my heart was *not* for sale.

I felt chilled, although I've never been the paranoid type, preferring to be optimistic and to expect the best. But I knew that if I didn't watch out, I'd grow afraid of every shifting shadow or sudden sound. Cressida probably started out self-confident and capable. But working as a model meant being told what to do and being pampered. Her agent took care of her career and her manager cushioned her day-to-day life. Gradually, Cressida came to rely on them, losing herself along the way.

But I wasn't going to lose myself, or my life. And I wouldn't simply wait around, wondering who was out to get me. I'd find out who was menacing me, even if it meant telling Cressida I was her clone.

Sure, she'd be shocked at first. But if Dolores was telling the truth about the stolen eggs, then Cressida had probably wondered if she had an unknown child. And she did, sort of. Only I was more than her child: I was like her. And when she realized this, our friendship would blossom into something special: family.

The truck slowed and parked in front of the Fergus house.

I was home, yet already planning to leave again. With a rush of excitement, I wondered when the limo would arrive to pick me up. I couldn't wait to talk with Cressida.

But when Chase and I entered the house, Professor Fergus met us at the door with a brown-paper-wrapped package in his hands and surprising news.

"Look what just arrived," he said as he gently cradled the book-size package. "It's from Reena, a.k.a. Cousin Tansy."

"What!" we both exclaimed.

The Professor nodded. "I haven't opened it yet. I thought I'd wait till all of us were together. But Eric is at a friend's house and Varina is doing homework research at the library."

I was dumbfounded by the package and couldn't tear my gaze from it. "What could it be?" I murmured. "Why would Reena/Tansy send us anything?"

"We'll find out soon enough," the Professor said patiently, reaching up to smooth his salt-and-pepper hair. "A few more hours won't make any difference."

"But I can't wait. I have to—" I halted, knowing he'd disapprove of my visit to Cressida, especially if he guessed I planned to tell her about the clone experiment. So my best course was to keep quiet for now and to make sure I was back in time for our meeting.

I heard the front door slam, then saw Eric and Starr

step into the foyer. They were holding hands, their gazes locked, and looking like the perfect couple, down to their identical blue shirts and jeans.

Professor Fergus quickly told Eric there would be a meeting when Varina returned.

"You're stuck here, Eric?" Starr's bright mauve lips puckered in a pout. "But we were going to go to a movie."

"We can go tomorrow night," Eric said.

"I guess." Starr still looked disappointed. "I was looking forward to spending all evening with you."

"Sorry." A helpless look crossed his face, as if he didn't have a clue how to appease Starr.

I turned and headed for my room, leaving the two lovebirds to smooth things out by themselves. I wanted to find out about the package from Reena, but I was anxious to meet with Cressida. Though getting away, I knew, could prove to be a real challenge. I'd watch for the limo from my window, then sneak out and hopefully return before anyone knew I was gone.

I hated deceiving the Professor, but I just had to find out what Cressida wanted to tell me.

Something about my future.

A short time later, I spied Cressida's limousine turning on our street. Quickly, I snuck out of my room. I heard low sounds from the living room and glimpsed Eric and Chase inside watching TV. The door to the Professor's office was shut, so he was probably working in there. Which left the coast clear for me to slip outside with no awkward explanations.

Chauffeur Leo politely opened the back door for me, and I scooted into the plush limo.

"Thanks for coming to get me," I told him.

"Miss Ray's orders. She's eager to see you."

"I feel the same about her. We have so much to talk about."

"I'm sure you do. Enjoy your ride." He gave a curt nod as he courteously closed my door.

The dividing window was up, so there was no further conversation. I wished I could ask him personal questions about Cressida. Since he'd been with her for over twenty years, I figured he must know her well. He could tell me what she was like as a young woman, why she and Jackson divorced, how bad her heart really was, and if Dolores was telling the truth about the frozen eggs.

With these questions and more swirling in my head, I leaned back and closed my eyes until we reached the hotel.

"This way, miss," the chauffeur said as he led me through the lobby to the bank of elevators. He moved swiftly, though rigidly, and I practically had to run to keep up with him.

We stepped inside the elevator and the chauffeur pushed the P button, for Penthouse Suite.

When the elevator door swooshed open, there was Cressida waiting for me. She grinned, held out her arms, and then enfolded me in a warm hug. Her hair smelled like strawberries and her touch was gentle. I felt a strong sense of connection, like I never wanted to let go.

"Come on inside and sit down," she told me. "Leo will wait in the lobby and give us a call when Jackson and Dolores return from dinner."

"Isn't Sarah Ann with them?"

"No. She's in her own hotel room watching TV. But she's a darling and never a bother anyway."

Cressida sat in an orange velvet chair at a small table and I sat opposite her, setting my cap down and smoothing my hair away from my face. "I'm glad to be here," I told her.

"Me too. Would you like anything to eat or drink?"

"Not yet. Maybe we should just talk." I clenched my hands, wondering how to bring up the topic of frozen eggs and clones.

"All right." Her dark eyes sparkled. "I've been bursting to tell you my idea."

"What?"

"Allison dear . . ." She reached out and wrapped her hands around mine. "I want you to stay with me. Permanently."

THIRTY-TWO

"Huh?" I gave her a puzzled look.

"Do you believe in fate?"

"Well, yeah. I think lots of unusual stuff is possible. But what does that have to do with anything?"

"It's not a coincidence you're so much like me."

I nodded. "Yeah. There's a reason."

"Fate. We were meant to be together." She squeezed my hands. "So be my protégée. Travel with me as my assistant and friend. I'll get a private tutor for you. And I'll teach you how to model so we can work together. It'll be so much fun."

"But Dolores and Jackson won't want me around."

"They'll change their minds. If not, that's their problem. Will you do it?"

The determination in her tone impressed me. And I looked down at our joined hands and felt such a strong sense of longing it nearly took my breath away. I loved my parents, but didn't have much in common with them. They didn't understand me, sending me away when I'd hoped they'd beg me to stay. But Cressida was more than a parent, and she wasn't sending me away.

She really wanted me.

Still, I didn't know how to respond. Modeling was okay, but not something I cared about. I *did* care about my clone cousins, and enjoyed living with them. Someday Sandee might even join us, and then we'd be a complete family. But this would never happen if I left.

I didn't know what I wanted.

"Allison, I know this must seem rushed to you." Cressida sipped from a bottle of sparkling water. "But I've always been the impulsive type."

"I'm kind of impulsive, too," I said with a smile. We were *so* much alike, it would have been spooky if I hadn't known the reason.

"When I decide on something, I just jump in and do it," Cressida went on.

"I usually do, too, but I can't decide about this so quickly. It's too important. . . ." My words trailed off as I battled with conflicting emotions.

"I know you aren't close to your family," she pointed out. "And I feel for you. But you can share my large family. I have five terrific siblings, a great father, and Mom is the old-fashioned type who loves to cook and sew. You'd love her."

Her mother was my mother, or maybe my grandmother. It would be great to meet her, to blend in with an instant family.

"I wish I could just say yes, but it's more complicated than that. I'm staying with some great people that I really care about. Besides . . ." I blew out a deep breath, then admitted, "This isn't what I thought we'd talk about. I thought maybe you knew about my past."

"What does your past have to do with anything?" Her brows arched with curiosity.

"It's not just my past. It's yours too."

I braced myself. Okay, this was it. Time to talk about clones and attempted murder.

But I didn't know where to start, so I blurted out, "Is it true your frozen eggs were stolen from a fertility clinic?"

Her dark eyes widened. "How did you hear about that?"

"Dolores said so."

"She told you *that*?"

"Not me. I heard her on the phone with Dominique Eszlinger."

"Dolores talked to the Mudslinger about *me*?" Her hands shook, nearly knocking over her drink.

"Yes. She sold the information for a lot of money. But is it true?"

"Yes, but it happened a long time ago. I can't believe Dolores would reveal something so painful to me."

"Well, she did. She also—" I sucked in a huge breath for courage. "She said I might be your daughter."

Cressida gasped, gripping the table for support.

"Are you okay? I—I'm sorry. I didn't want to upset you."

"My daughter?" she whispered, staring at me with dark, shocked eyes. "No. It can't be. I knew the eggs were gone, but I thought they'd been destroyed."

"At least one survived, but not in the way you'd think. I mean, I'm not your daughter. I'm more than that," I said firmly. "I have a special connection with you."

As I paused to find the proper words, there was a sudden rap at the door. "Miss Ray, open up. It's Leo."

"Not now," she yelled.

"It's important."

"Oh, all right," she said crossly. To me she added, "We'll continue this in a moment."

Then she went to the door. "Okay, Leo. What's up?"

"Dolores is back."

"I don't care," she said with an impatient shake of her head. "Tell her to leave me alone. Say I'm sleeping or in the shower. Whatever works."

"But she isn't alone." He gave his employer a concerned look. "Bob Nelson is with her."

"My doctor? Dr. Nelson left his practice to come all the way from L.A.? How dare Dolores contact him behind my back? First the Mudslinger and now this. She's gone too far."

"She'll be here soon," he warned. "Miss Beaumont should leave or it could be awkward. I'll take her home."

"But we haven't finished talking," Cressida complained.

"I'll hide in the bedroom," I suggested.

"That's too obvious." Cressida touched her finger to her chin, thinking for a moment. "I have a better idea. You can go to Sarah Ann's room. Tell her I sent you."

"I'll escort her," Leo offered.

"Please do. And I'll call when the coast is clear."

"I still don't like running off, but I guess I'll go," I said reluctantly.

I followed the chauffeur out of the room and into the elevator. His shoulders were tense and his hands were clenched, probably, I figured, because he was worried about Cressida's health.

He reached out to the panel on the wall and punched in the G.

"I thought Sarah Ann's room was just a few floors down. Why are we going to the garage?"

"Sarah Ann left a package in the limo. I forgot to get it earlier. It'll only take a moment."

"Okay." I wondered if the package had anything to do with Sarah Ann's new agent.

The elevator moved down in a smooth rush of speed, then stopped at the garage level. It was a dark underground space, dank and eerily quiet except for a few slow-moving cars. Way off in a corner, I spotted the limousine. It was parked by an exit.

"I'll wait here," I told Leo.

"No. I don't think so." He stared at me with cold eyes,

then whipped his hand from his pocket. A small black object was curled tightly in his fingers.

"What!" I gasped.

"You're coming with me." He aimed the gun at me and spoke in a chilling tone. "Now."

THIRTY-THREE

"What's going on?" I choked out, unable to believe this was really happening. "Is this a sick joke?"

"I don't joke. Shut up." He poked the hard, deadly gun into my back. "Or you're dead now."

"Why—why me?"

"I said shut up." The gun jabbed viciously. "This is your own fault. I warned you."

"With the note in my locker?" I guessed, looking around for someone to help. There were cars moving a few rows away, but no one slowed or paid attention to a young girl with a man who could have been her adoring grandfather.

"Move," he ordered, pushing me forward. "Go to the limo."

"Why?" I demanded. "So you can kill me there?"

"Doesn't matter where. Move." He grabbed my shoulder with his free hand, digging in. Hard.

And I moved.

Each step was agony, bringing me closer to certain death. Tears came to my eyes, and I fought panic. I wanted to run, scream, fight, but I could barely move—I was numb with terror. Even incredible strength like mine, I knew, couldn't fight a bullet. I had to bide my time, wait for a chance to escape.

It was my only hope.

We were nearing the limo, only a dozen cars away. *Think, Allison*, I urged myself. *Do something. Stall. Get him talking.*

"Were you the guy in the orange cap on the construction site who dropped the roof shakes?" I asked in a rush of words.

"That was your first warning."

"Did you also trap me in that hole? It was you, wasn't it?"

"I don't know how you got out," he growled. "I had a devil of a time moving that concrete."

"And you shot at me in the park?"

"You got lucky there." He scowled. "I seldom miss."

I shivered and glanced around desperately for an escape route, but there was none.

We were only four cars from the limo now, and I knew that when we reached it, my life was over. But would he risk firing a gun in such an enclosed place? Someone was bound to hear.

He didn't stop at the limo. Instead he pushed me forward, to the door marked Exit.

"W-where are we going?"

"Open the door," he ordered, the gun roughly digging into my back.

With trembling hands, I reached out and grasped the knob. I twisted and pulled. Though it was a heavy door, I opened it easily.

We went into a narrow hallway, a deserted passage of some kind where my echoing footsteps were the only sound. I swallowed hard. Had I just entered my own coffin?

Leo spun me around, grabbed my arm, and pointed

the gun at my chest. He really *was* going to kill me. I could read intent on his face. He regarded me as if I was less than human, an insect to be squished. My life had no value to him, except as an inconvenience.

"Don't," I pleaded in a ragged whisper. "Please, you don't want to do this."

"I don't want to, but I have to. In the army, I had many unpleasant duties, which I fulfilled without hesitation. Of course, once I retired I thought I was done with killing—until you showed up," he spat out. "You almost ruined everything."

"I—I didn't mean to." I couldn't tear my gaze away from the black gun pointed at my chest. So small, and possibly the last thing I would ever see.

A bizarre thought struck me, and I cried, "Why are you aiming there? It doesn't make sense. You'll destroy my heart."

"What are you babbling about?"

"My heart. Isn't that why you want to kill me?" I half-sobbed. "To replace Cressida's heart with mine?"

"You're crazy." His brows knitted together, his expression switching from cold to confused. "Making up wild stories won't help."

"I'm not making up anything. I—I thought that's why you wanted to kill me, because I'm Cressida's clone."

"That *is* why. To keep you from telling her. When I sold her frozen eggs to Dr. Victor, he told me some wild story about cloning people. But I didn't believe that sci-fi garbage. I figured it would never work." His frown deepened. "Then you sent that letter and I saw your picture. I knew that doctor had been serious. And I had to insure that Miss Ray never learned the truth."

"Why?"

"Because I sold her out. I hated betraying her, but I needed money for gambling debts, and Dr. Victor was offering plenty."

"You did it? I—I never guessed. But why—why kill me?"

"If Miss Ray figured out that I betrayed her, she'd hate me. And I'd rather die. She's like an angel, the only good thing in my life. And no one is going to turn her against me."

"That's the reason for the murder attempts? To shut me up, not to take my heart?" I blinked in astonishment. "But Dolores said Cressida would need a heart transplant."

"You're lying. She isn't sick, just overworked. If she needed a transplant, she would have told me."

"Maybe she didn't want to worry you." *Keep him talking,* I thought desperately. I could feel my strength growing, bursting for release. If only he'd put that gun down. "I'm Cressida's clone, so you know we're alike. And I don't always tell my friends things that will worry them. Cressida would protect her friends, too."

"She really needs a transplant?" he asked hoarsely. "She's dying?"

He stared at me in shock, his skin turning pale and his hand shaking. It was my chance, and I didn't hesitate.

Summoning all my strength, I sprang forward. I grabbed the wrist of his gun hand. Then I squeezed hard, my grip as strong as steel. He cried out in pain. And the gun clattered to the ground.

I grabbed his other arm and then gave him a mighty shove into the air. He flew high and far, crashing to the ground yards away. My terror changed to shaky relief. He couldn't hurt me anymore.

The door behind us jerked open, sending cold air swooshing in. I coughed, as if reality were shaking me. And I heard a horrified gasp.

I twisted my head to look behind and saw Cressida standing there with a stunned expression.

"Allison!" she exclaimed in a shrill voice. "What have you done to Leo?"

THIRTY-FOUR

I stared at Cressida, then looked back to Leo. He was huddling against the wall, holding one arm at an odd angle like it was broken. Blood trickled down his nose and he was sobbing, "I'm so, so sorry. Sorry."

Cressida just stared, her face ashen.

"Cressida," I sobbed. "Thank God you came."

"You—you left this in the room." Her hand shook as she held out my yellow cap to me. "I came to give it to you, but you weren't in Sarah Ann's room. I checked Leo's room, too, and nothing. So I came down here. . . ." Her voice trailed off. "I can't believe this."

"Me either." My head throbbed from adrenaline and terror. But as the terror ebbed away and my heartbeat slowed, all I saw was a pitiful old man. "He tried to kill me."

"I know." Cressida regarded both of us through stricken eyes. "I—I heard."

"So you know I'm your clone?"

She nodded, but didn't say anything.

I stood there anxiously, yearning for her to put her

arms around me and tell me everything would be fine. I'd nearly been killed, and still felt shaken. She would understand how I felt, because we were the same.

But instead she stepped past me, not even meeting my gaze. Tears streamed down her cheeks as she knelt by Leo. She put her arms around him, cradling him like a child, and told him everything would be okay. "No matter what you've done," she murmured, "I'm here for you, like you've always been there for me."

"Not always. I—I lied. Dolores didn't call Dr. Nelson," he whimpered. "And I lied about other things, too."

"It's okay."

"I—I was desperate. She was going to tell you."

"It doesn't matter." She stroked his gray hair. "You're my dear friend, and I care about you."

"I—I don't deserve it."

With a strangled cry, he pushed away from her and jumped to his feet. Moaning, he held his injured arm, a wild look on his face. Before I knew what was happening, he rushed past me and ran out the door.

Cressida was up on her feet, racing after him, calling his name and begging him to come back. She didn't even glance at me. It was her longtime friend she cared about, not her genetic double.

I meant nothing to her.

And I never would.

THIRTY-FIVE

The next moments were like a nightmare.

Leo drove off in the limousine, burning rubber and screeching away while Cressida pleaded with him to come back.

When I went over to Cressida to console her, to tell her everything would be okay, she shook me off with a cold stare.

"I can't deal with you right now" was all she said.

Then she hurried toward the elevators.

I stood there, uncertain what to do. Call the police? Go after Cressida? Go home?

I knew a murder attempt should be reported, but it would be my word against Leo's. Or even worse—my word against Leo's and Cressida's. She'd made it clear where her loyalty lay.

So I found a phone and called Professor Fergus.

A while later, I was back home, totally exhausted and emotionally drained. I thought about how I had made the mistake of keeping secrets to protect people. I wasn't going to make that mistake again.

Varina was home by now, so I was able to tell my three clone cousins and the Professor about my horrifying near-death experience with Cressida's chauffeur. When I finished, I tensed, waiting for their anger at my recklessness. But instead, they offered sympathy and concern. I'd acted stupidly, and yet they still stood by me. Like a family.

"At least it's over now." Varina reached out to give me a tight, caring hug. "I'm so glad you're safe."

"Me too. But I wasn't sure for a while. He really wanted to kill me. And he almost did."

"That jerk needs to be taken care of," Chase said furiously. "You can't just let him get away."

"I know," I admitted. "But it would be my word against his."

"Just thinking about it scares me. You're like my sister, and I'd die if anything happened to you." Varina hugged me again, and I held on to her. It occurred to me that Varina, who didn't share my DNA, had spoken all the words I'd expected from Cressida.

Then I said I didn't want to talk about it right now. "Have you opened the package from Tansy yet?" I asked.

"No," Professor Fergus answered. "We were waiting for you."

"I'm here now."

We went downstairs to the living room. The Professor eased himself into the cushy reclining chair, with one hand reaching out to rest on the top of his cane. I sat next to Eric on the couch. And when Varina scooted close to Chase on the love seat, he reached out to hold her hand. The smile they shared was intimate and sizzling with electricity. Maybe Chase was finally getting smart and noticing her.

Professor Fergus slowly unwrapped the package, the torn paper sliding as quietly as a shadow to the carpeted floor. And the rest of us watched, waiting, breathless with curiosity.

Inside was a plain oblong wooden box.

There was a brief note on the front which said:

Mr. Fergus,
My cousin asked me to give you this farewell gift. I have cared for her in secret for many years, healing both physical and emotional wounds. She regretted experimenting on babies and also worried Dr. V would get the formula from her and misuse it. Now she's left to start a new life. Please don't try to find her or contact me again. Tansy.

Professor Fergus sighed and murmured, "Jessica."

Then he studied the polished mahogany jewel box. Carved onto the top was the figure of a lovely, ethereal woman. Her name, Pandora, was etched across her flowing skirt.

"It's beautiful!" I exclaimed. "What's inside?"

"I don't know." He lifted the wooden box's curved lid, and I peered inside.

"Nothing!" I exclaimed.

Varina wrinkled her brow and asked, "But why would she send you an empty box?"

"I have no idea," her uncle replied sadly.

"Maybe she's moving to a town called Pandora," Chase said.

"Or with a friend named Pandora," Eric added.

"The box itself could be a clue," Chase pointed out.

"Yeah. A clue I can check out," Eric said with a thoughtful expression. He took off his glasses and faced the carved box. His black eyes glazed over in a mesmerizing stare.

"Yes!" he suddenly cried, grabbing his glasses and slipping them back on. "There is something. Inside."

"But it's empty," the Professor insisted.

"Or so it seems." Eric crossed the room. "Uncle Jim, may I have the box?"

"Of course." He handed it to Eric.

Surprisingly, Eric turned and gave the box to me. "Take it, Allison." Then he whispered what he wanted me to do.

Firmly grasping the lovely carved box, I pressed on the bottom. I squeezed hard, harder, and even harder—until there was a sharp cracking sound.

"You broke it!" Varina accused. "Allison, can't you control your strength?"

I just grinned, then felt among the cracked bits of wood until I found the slim rectangular object hidden in the box. It was encased in foil, and slowly I unwrapped it. Then, with a smile, I held out a tape cassette.

"A secret compartment. Wonderful, Allison!" Professor Fergus exulted. "You did it!"

"Not me. Eric. His super sight found the cassette. I just helped retrieve it," I said.

Professor Fergus left to retrieve a tape player, then returned a few moments later. My heart jumped when the tape came on and I heard the soft voice of a woman.

"That's her!" Varina cried, tears filling her eyes. "Jessica of my dreams."

I felt a lump in my throat, especially when I saw tears streaming down Varina's face. I understood how she felt. In a way, we'd both found our DNA mothers, only to lose them.

Eric gave her a doubtful glance, but didn't say anything.

The room grew quiet, except for Jessica's voice.

"Hello, Jim," she began. "You're a special man, and if I hadn't been married to my research, I might have accepted your proposal and been the wife you deserved. Only instead of helping people with science, I ended up hurting those I cared for the most." There was a pause, a low sob, and then she continued, "Tell the children that I'm sorry for running away from them at Tansy's shop. But I panicked. I—I couldn't face them . . . especially Varina. It's safer to stay out of your lives. Don't try to find me. The following information is something I trust only you with; it's both a farewell gift and a curse."

Then she began to recite complicated medical terms and instructions. Professor Fergus gasped, then hurriedly reached over to shut off the tape.

"Am I crazy or is that what I think it is?" Varina gave her uncle an astonished look.

"You're not crazy." He rubbed his beard and frowned. "The Enhance-X25 formula."

After a casual dinner of turkey sandwiches and clam chowder, I joined Eric in the living room to watch some sitcoms on TV. It felt good to sit back and relax as if we were typical kids just hanging out on a Friday evening.

But during a commercial, there was a short mention of upcoming news, and a familiar name caught my attention.

". . . Cressida Ray, a successful model."

"What about Cressida?" I exclaimed. "Did you hear that, Eric? Something's happened to Cressida!"

"Slow down and listen." Eric put a calming arm around me. "News reports always overdramatize things. I'm sure it's nothing bad."

But he was wrong.

I scooted closer to the TV.

"Tonight on our eleven o'clock news," the twenty-something newscaster went on, "we'll give you more details about this tragic car accident that appears to be a suicide. A limousine belonging to Ms. Ray drove off a steep cliff earlier today. The sole occupant was killed instantly: a longtime employee of Ms. Ray. Her chauffeur, Leonard Addison."

THIRTY-SIX

While my friends were at the Sadie Hawkins Dance a week later, I sat alone in the living room watching TV. Well, not actually watching, My mind was wandering and for the zillionth time I reread the letter in my lap.

It had arrived today.

From Cressida.

"Allison," the letter began. No "dear" or "darling" or other warm salutation. Simply my name.

Things are very sad for me right now, but I felt I owed you an explanation.

I'm sorry things didn't work out. Although we have some things in common, we're really quite different.

My health has improved since I've stopped working so hard. And the doctor says if I continue to improve, my heart will keep on ticking for a long time.

Sarah Ann wanted me to say "Hi," and let you know her career is going wonderfully. Her agent is much sharper than her father, Jackson, ever was, and I predict she'll be on a runway in Paris within a year. I'm giving her some tips, and in return she's helping me out in the office.

You were right about Dolores selling news to Dominique. She'd been doing it for years, making up lies to keep my name in the press and to earn extra money. Naturally, I had to let her go.

So life changes, and I am forced to change with it. But I can only take a few changes at a time. And while I'm glad we met, please don't contact me again.

I hope you enjoy the enclosed picture.

Good luck with the hammers and nails.

Cressida

I stared at the 8×10 photograph of the two of us, side by side, alike and yet two completely different people. Cressida was smiling at me as we posed on playground swings. And I was smiling back with a wistful expression.

I sighed. Cressida wasn't comfortable with me. Maybe Leo was the reason, but I had a feeling she couldn't deal with having a clone.

And I knew I'd never see her again.

But that was okay. I had special friends who might not share my DNA, but who were there when I needed them. Family had a lot of definitions these days; I'd just make up my own as I went along. Four clones and an uncle were a nice start. I might even start calling the Professor "Uncle Jim."

Maybe.

The front door burst open and I quickly tucked my letter back in the envelope as Eric, Starr, Varina, and Chase rushed inside. They were laughing. Eric had his arm draped over Starr's shoulders, and Varina glowed with delight, probably because Chase was holding her hand.

Clearly, the dance had been a success.

"You should have gone," Varina told me, then leaned over to whisper into my ear, "Chase said I was special to him and then kissed me. It was wonderful!"

I nodded and gave her a thumbs-up.

Then I turned to Starr, who was raving about the dance. "The decorations were gorgeous, the band was way hot, and the refreshments were delicious."

"Those little cookies with strawberry drops in them were the best," Eric said.

"They were good, but the ice-cream punch was better." Starr's beads jangled as she scooted onto the couch beside Eric. "You missed a good one, Allison. Your fave guy was there, too."

"Who?" I leaned forward curiously.

"Who else?" Starr laughed. "Dustin. That boy may have some attitude problems, but he can sure dance."

"You can have him," I teased.

"Nope. She's all mine," Eric said, giving Starr a possessive squeeze.

Starr returned the squeeze, then went into a detailed description of who was at the dance, what they wore, and how some of them misbehaved. She set us all laughing.

But we stopped instantly at the sound of an odd thud near the front door.

"What was that?" Chase asked, touching his ear. "A knock?"

"Beats me," Eric said with a shrug.

"Let's find out." I stood and went to the door, with Chase and Varina beside me and Eric and Starr trailing.

Reaching out, I pulled open the door.

A girl with short blond-streaked black hair and an odd silver band around her ankle had collapsed on the doorstep. There were dark bruises and bloody cuts on her skin, as if someone had beaten her up, then dumped her like garbage.

"It's *her*!" Chase gasped as he rushed forward and knelt by the girl. He gently pushed back her bangs and stared into her unconscious face. "Oh, no," he exclaimed softly. "Sandee! Who did this to you?"

ABOUT THE AUTHOR

Linda Joy Singleton lives on three acres near Sacramento, California, with her supportive husband, David, and two terrific teens, Melissa and Andy. She has a barnyard of animals, including horses, pigs, cats, dogs, and a goat. One of the newest additions in her family is a dog named Renegade.

She's the author of over twenty juvenile novels, as well as numerous short "chiller" stories. Links to these stories and other information about the author can be found at her website: http://www.geocities.com/Athens/Acropolis/4815.